TYCOON TAKES REVENGE

ANNA DePALO

Published by Silhouette Books
America's Publisher of Contemporary Romance

SILHOUETTE BOOKS

ISBN 0-373-76697-1

TYCOON TAKES REVENGE

Visit Silhouette Books at www.eHarlequin.com

Printed in U.S.A.

Noah's Pl

So Why Was She Tempted?

Kayla considered him a moment. "What would be the terms of our dating?"

She saw the flare of gratification in his eyes, but he quickly banked it. "Terms?"

"There has to be a time limit," she said firmly.

"Make your best offer," he countered.

"Two weeks."

He shook his head. "Six. These things take time."

"Let's split the difference," she countered. "Four. It shouldn't take long to repair the damage of having to be seen with you in public."

"A pleasure doing business with you." He closed the space between them and held out his hand.

Relief, followed by panic, washed through her. She took his hand, felt her own engulfed in his, and experienced a surge of sensation. She started to draw away, but he pulled her closer. He lifted her chin with his free hand and she had just a moment to lower her eyelids before he brushed her lips with his.

Dear Reader,

Celebrate the conclusion of 2005 with the six fabulous novels available this month from Silhouette Desire. You won't be able to put down the scintillating finale to DYNASTIES: THE ASHTONS once you start reading Barbara McCauley's *Name Your Price*. He believes she was bought off by his father...she can't fathom his lack of trust. Neither can deny the passion still pulsing between them.

We are so excited to have Caroline Cross back writing for Desire...and with a brand-new miniseries, MEN OF STEELE. In *Trust Me,* reunited lovers have more to deal with than just relationship troubles—they are running for their lives. Kristi Gold kicks one out of the corral as she wraps up TEXAS CATTLEMAN'S CLUB: THE SECRET DIARY with her story of secrets and scandals, *A Most Shocking Revelation.*

Enjoy the holiday cheer found in Joan Elliott Pickart's *A Bride by Christmas,* the story of a wedding planner who believes she's jinxed never to be a bride herself. Anna DePalo is back with another millionaire playboy who finally meets his match, in *Tycoon Takes Revenge.* And finally, welcome brand-new author Jan Colley to the Desire lineup with *Trophy Wives,* a story of lies and seduction not to be missed.

Be sure to come back next month when we launch a new and fantastic twelve-book family dynasty, THE ELLIOTTS.

Melissa Jeglinski

Melissa Jeglinski
Senior Editor
Silhouette Books

Please address questions and book requests to:
Silhouette Reader Service
U.S.: 3010 Walden Ave., P.O. Box 1325, Buffalo, NY 14269
Canadian: P.O. Box 609, Fort Erie, Ont. L2A 5X3

Books by Anna DePalo

Silhouette Desire

Having the Tycoon's Baby #1530
Under the Tycoon's Protection #1643
Tycoon Takes Revenge #1697

ANNA DePALO

A lifelong book lover, Anna discovered that she was a writer at heart when she realized that not everyone travels around with a full cast of characters in their head. She has lived in Italy and England, learned to speak French, graduated from Harvard, earned graduate degrees in political science and law, forgotten how to speak French and married her own dashing hero.

Anna has been an intellectual-property lawyer in New York City. She loves traveling, reading, writing, old movies, chocolate and Italian (which she hasn't forgotten how to speak, thanks to her extended Italian family). She's thrilled to be writing for Silhouette. Readers can visit her at www.annadepalo.com.

For my sister, Pina,
and my cousin Anna Dagostino,
who've always been there for me

One

Gossip is news running ahead of itself in a red satin dress.
—*Columnist Liz Smith*

Smooth, moneyed and used to having things fall in his lap.

In short, Kayla thought disdainfully, as she watched him move toward her with a thin gloss of civility, he was everything that her family history had taught her to avoid.

Noah Whittaker. She'd spotted him instantly when she'd arrived at the cocktail party tonight at one of Boston's finer hotels to celebrate a retired Formula One race-car driver's newly published autobiography.

Her headline about Noah in that morning's *Boston*

Sentinel flashed through her mind: Caught with Fluffy, Huffy Calls It Quits. Will Buffy the Man Slayer Be Next for Noah?

She supposed he hadn't liked her story one bit. But she didn't make the news, she just reported it. And he gave her plenty of material to work with. He had, in fact, become a popular figure in her column.

And writing about him was easy. She knew his type. He acted as if the world were his cocktail, served up dry with a twist just for him, exactly as her biological father did.

She watched him approach and pushed aside the irritating twinge of nervousness. *She had nothing to be nervous about.*

She knew that, for *some* women, thoughts of sin and Noah Whittaker went hand in hand. But she'd been inoculated at birth against the players of the world—though she could dispassionately assess the attraction: Noah's hair, closely cropped but thick, looked as if he dried it with a blow-dryer set on scorch, its shade a burnished bronze. Over six feet tall, he had the honed body of an athlete. He'd had a brief but meteoric career as a race-car driver, though these days, he was better known as a vice president of Whittaker Enterprises, the family conglomerate in Carlyle, near Boston.

Noah stopped in front of her. "Kayla Jones, right?" He paused for a moment, his face all lean, hard planes of masculinity. "Or should I say," he added, his tone betraying a hint of derision, "Ms. Rumor-Has-It?"

Her chin came up. If he thought to faze her, he had

another thing coming. She'd gotten plenty of practice handling barbs from the pampered and privileged at the fancy prep school she'd attended on scholarship. "That's right. It's nice of you to remember."

One side of his mouth quirked up. "Hard to forget when you've been wielding a machete all over my social life. Or is that part of your job description as the *Boston Sentinel*'s resident gossip columnist?"

Her shoulders stiffened. They'd seen each other a few times at various social events, but this was the first time he'd deigned to speak with her personally. "I prefer the term *society columnist*. I write for the style section of the *Sentinel*."

"Is that what they're calling the fiction part of the paper these days?"

She attempted a dismissive laugh. "If I hadn't heard that line before from more people than I can count, I'd say you were trying to insult me."

He cocked his head, seeming to consider her question. "That depends. Are you trying to spread lies about me, or is that just a nice little fringe benefit in your line of work?"

"For your information, all my columns are carefully researched and my sources checked for reliability."

"Obviously you need to work harder."

"Are we by chance discussing my column in today's paper?"

"Oh, yeah, we're discussing that all right. And last week's column. And the one before that. One guess as to what they all have in common."

"There's no need to descend into sarcasm," she said. "I'm aware of how often I've mentioned you in my column."

"Are you?" he asked silkily. "And are you also aware it's your fault that Eve Bernard—or as you've referred to her, Huffy—broke up with me?"

From what she'd heard, Eve had done more than break up with him. According to eyewitnesses with whom she'd spoken, Eve had delivered the news—along with a slap to the face—in the presence of dozens of departing guests at a glittering banquet on Saturday night. A *Sentinel* photographer had gotten a great shot of Noah, glowering at Eve and holding her by the forearms.

But what did he mean it was *her* fault?

"As a result of my column?" she asked with skepticism. "Don't you mean as a result of your cavorting with Fluffy?" At his sardonic look, she caught herself. "I mean, Cecily?"

He chuckled cynically. "Cavorting? My, my, what colorful language you society columnists use. All the better to write innuendo, I suppose?"

She tossed her head. "Whatever," she retorted, dropping all pretense of politeness. Out of the corner of her eye, she noticed other guests had begun to throw curious glances their way. "There was a photo of you and Cecily kissing outside the Kirkland Club."

"And we all know a picture is worth a thousand words, right?" he responded. "Or, in this case, a thousand lies. In fact, if you had done some inquiring instead of relying on that shot that your photographer snapped, you would have discovered that Cecily caught me by surprise with that kiss."

"How nice for you."

He ignored her. "You see, Cecily has this weird idea that making the gossip columns will bolster her fledgling acting career—and so much the better if the guy on her arm happens to be rich or famous. So she plastered herself to me the minute she spotted the *Sentinel*'s photographer."

"Perhaps then," she said sweetly, "you should reconsider the risk of dating publicity-seeking aspiring actresses. Or, for that matter, intellectually challenged models. And, hmm—" she pretended to consider for an instant, tilting her head "—I seem to recall at least one ruthless reality-show contestant as well."

"Oh?" he responded, letting his gaze rake over her from head to toe. "Considering that the field doesn't yet include any gossip columnists, I don't think my tastes can be called into question."

"From what I've been able to see, your *tastes* can best be described as blond, platinum-blond and strawberry-blond."

"Are you calling me shallow?"

"If the shoe fits," she retorted.

He shook his head. "So young and yet so bitter."

Bitter? No, she was *cautious*, but that's how a single woman budgeting to make rent payments had to be. And how the product of a fling between a slick, social-climbing financier and his young college intern knew to be. But then *Mr. Playboy Whittaker* didn't have a clue about the struggles of ordinary people.

Aloud, she countered, "We journalists have jobs that require us to *think*, and thinking doesn't appear to be high on your list of criteria for a girlfriend."

"Whether it is or not isn't anyone's business but mine," he responded.

"For your information, I didn't just rely on the photo. I called Huff—I mean, Eve—about it and she confirmed she was planning to break up with you over the, ah, incident."

"That's because Eve was thinking of her public image. She believed me when I said your column had miscon-strued things because she knows Cecily is a publicity hound. But, as she put it, publicly she had to at least look like she was punishing me for being a naughty boy."

Kayla felt her lips twitch. "Well, that's not my fault, is it?"

"It *is* your fault," he disagreed. "You're printing sa-lacious gossip and you're wreaking havoc on my so-cial life."

"So find yourself another aspiring starlet," she re-torted. "In fact, I think Buffy the Man Slayer is between men these days."

"Right, and that's another thing," he said tightly. "I don't need you trying to line up dates for me. Particu-larly not with someone known as a barracuda in heels."

"Now that's not nice." She spread her hands in an ex-pansive gesture. "You should consider expanding your horizons."

He braced an arm on the wall near her head and she took an involuntary step back. He leaned in, his gaze, green and grim, boring into hers. "You know, I wonder why you consider me such a fascinating subject. Is it because you wish you were one of those women I date?"

"Don't be absurd," she snapped.

He gave her a slow once-over, dwelling on her ringless hand and letting his eyes linger on her chest before coming back to meet her outraged expression. "You do appear a little uptight. What's the matter? Wish your life had a little more *zing* in it?"

"No thanks. My mother taught me to stay away from the players among men."

"Ah," he said. "Now we're getting somewhere. The intrepid reporter is repressed."

"This isn't about me," she said coldly. *What nerve.* He knew nothing about her life. *Nothing.*

"So, you have no problems dishing about others' lives, but yours is off-limits, is that it?"

"There's nothing to dish about," she retorted. "I don't have anything as interesting as a fatal racing accident in my past!"

The minute she blurted the rejoinder, she winced inwardly, realizing she may have gone too far. He might be a first-class jerk who believed his money and his family name would get him out of any predicament, but she didn't need to throw a terrible tragedy in his face.

His face turned stony and he straightened. "Be glad you don't."

"Excuse me," she said, brushing past him and hurrying for the nearest exit.

Noah stared broodingly at Kayla's retreating back. Damn.

"Problems?"

Turning, he noticed Sybil LaBreck, gossip columnist for the *Boston World,* standing behind him.

"Yeah. A little lovers' spat," he replied sarcastically.

Sybil's eyes widened, and Noah realized she'd taken his flippant comment seriously.

Sybil was Kayla's biggest rival among local gossip columnists. In her late fifties, Sybil looked like an updated version of Mrs. Santa Claus, but she could shovel the dirt with the best of them.

Sybil looked perplexed. "But you've been seen everywhere with that model—what's her name?—Eve."

Noah was about to tell Sybil that he'd been joking, but he suddenly realized he'd been handed a golden opportunity to even the score with Kayla. "The so-called relationship with Eve was just a smoke screen, a way to throw the paparazzi off the scent. Eve got a little publicity out of the arrangement, and Kayla and I got a little privacy. It was perfect."

"But only last week Eve was seen slapping you for cheating on her!" Sybil blurted before seeming to catch herself.

"Really?" Noah said, raising an eyebrow while privately relishing the thought of the headline in Sybil's column tomorrow. "It was a great way to signal the end of our pretend relationship for the benefit of the press, wasn't it?"

Sybil opened her mouth—in all likelihood to probe for more details—but he cut her off smoothly. "Excuse me." He let his eyes focus on a spot across the room. "I just spotted someone I need to say hello to."

"Of course," Sybil said, stepping aside.

He chanced a glance at her out of the corner of his eye as he moved past: she looked like the cat that had swallowed the canary.

As he headed to the bar at the far side of the room, he pondered again about his problem with Ms. Rumor-Has-It. If newspapers were printed in color, he thought to himself disgustedly, Kayla's column would be nothing but a series of hot-pink exclamation points. It had the same breathless quality as the gossip that sorority sisters shared over drying nail polish.

Of course, her column had nothing on the woman herself. Tonight she'd been wearing a clingy black cocktail dress that revealed a tantalizing bit of her full chest and a fair expanse of her shapely legs, her honey-blond hair hanging in a smooth curtain past her shoulders. Her eyes were large and wide set but balanced by lips that were lushly curved. Under other circumstances, she'd have been exactly his type—blond, busty and beautiful.

Still, even the attractive packaging couldn't obscure the fact that the woman was a menace. And he'd had enough. More than enough.

His reputation as the playboy Whittaker brother

made him a favorite of the press as well as the object of more than a little ribbing from his older brothers, Quentin and Matt, and his younger sister, Allison.

But the truth was that he worked damned hard in his position as vice president of product development for Whittaker Enterprises, the family business started by his father, James. His degree from the prestigious Massachusetts Institute of Technology was put to excellent use in his capacity as head of Whittaker's computer business.

If he liked to consort with models and actresses when he was let out of his prison cell—uh, office—well, he wasn't going to begrudge himself some fun. Besides, there was a worldwide shortage in decent-looking computer geeks like himself.

Frowning, he ordered a cocktail. Kayla had some gall taunting him with the car accident that had marked the end of his career racing Indy cars. God knew, if he could take back the accident that had killed another driver, he would. Didn't everyone understand that? Couldn't the press that had plagued him after the accident comprehend that?

His physical scars had healed but the emotional scars on his soul would never go away.

Turning away from the bar, he took a sip of his drink and thought again that it would be a shame to miss Kayla's reaction to Sybil's column in the morning.

But then again... A smile rose to his lips.

Reaching into the pocket of his pants, he pulled out his cell phone. The number he wanted was already programmed in, having been used both before and after countless dates: Bloomsville Florists.

The following morning, Kayla's first sign that something was wrong was the large bouquet of red roses parked on her desk in her cubicle at the *Boston Sentinel*'s headquarters.

At first she thought there must have been some mistake. She glanced around the office, then put her purse down and reached for the note that was tucked among the flowers.

After pulling the card from the envelope, she scanned the contents: "Kayla, thanks for a wonderful evening."

Confused, she turned the card over and then looked at the envelope, but there was no further clue as to who had sent the flowers and why—not even the name of a florist.

Hmm, interesting. Who could have sent the bouquet? She hadn't had a date in a couple of months, ever since she'd gone out with a radio-show producer before quickly deciding they had no chemistry.

Frowning, she sat down and logged onto her computer. She'd e-mail the receptionist; every visitor had to sign in at the front desk.

Out of habit, however, she first surfed to the news sites to check out the day's headlines and, more importantly, to scan the society pages. She made it a practice to read her rivals' gossip columns just to keep up with what the competition was doing.

When she got to the *Boston World*'s gossip page,

Sybil LaBreck's years-old, black-and-white photo stared back at her along with the headline Dangerous Liaisons: Noah Whittaker's Secret Relationship with Gossip Maven Kayla Jones, aka Ms. Rumor-Has-It.

She froze, blinked, and then stared.

No. But the headline was still there, staring at her, taunting her.

She scanned the rest of the article while a sickening feeling settled in the pit of her stomach.

Sybil alleged that Noah and Ms. Rumor-Has-It had been secretly involved for some time. The column went on to disclose a lovers' row that they'd had at the book-launch party last night. It ended by toying with the delicious possibility that Kayla's skewering of the millionaire playboy in her column had been a smoke screen for her own clandestine relationship with him.

Kayla's mind raced. Had Sybil witnessed her argument with Noah last night and wrongly concluded she'd been privy to a lovers' spat? Or—a more ominous thought intruded—had someone led Sybil to believe it *was* a lovers' spat?

She looked up from her computer screen and caught one of the *Sentinel*'s health columnists giving her a curious look. Had Sybil's headline already been making the rounds?

Kayla's eyes went to the flower bouquet again. Now that she'd read Sybil's headline, the flowers suddenly made sense.

Noah. The rat. Whether he'd started the flames or was just fanning them, she had a thing or two to tell him.

Using the Internet, she located the main number for Whittaker Enterprises. Once she dialed it, she was quickly transferred to Noah's secretary.

"May I ask who is calling?" the secretary intoned once Kayla had asked to speak with Noah.

"It's Kayla Jones."

"I'm sorry, Ms. Jones, but Mr. Whittaker isn't in the office yet this morning. May I take a message?"

He wasn't in the office yet? Probably due to his late-night carousing, she thought acidly. Her eyes strayed to the clock on the wall, which indicated it was just after nine.

As she looked down and started to tell Noah's secretary that she'd call back later, her gaze landed on the man striding toward her.

Noah Whittaker, smiling sunnily.

"Never mind," she said absently into the receiver. "I've found him." She couldn't believe he had the nerve to show up at her office! Planning to milk this baseless rumor for all it was worth, was he?

She hung up and straightened, rising from her chair just as Noah came to a stop in front of her.

He nodded to the impressive arrangement of red roses. "Glad to see I got my money's worth."

"You snake." She kept her voice low, not caring that her tone sounded furtive. The last thing she needed was for someone at the *Sentinel* to overhear her conversation. Fortunately, it was still early enough that a lot of the staff hadn't rolled in yet.

Noah chuckled. "Now is that any way to thank the guy who's come to apologize for our lovers' quarrel?"

"You know it was no such thing!" she exclaimed in a low tone, catching another curious look from the *Sentinel*'s health columnist.

"I suppose," he returned placidly, "you're about to express outrage and claim bloody retribution."

She looked at him. He seemed so smug, and he was so infuriating. "You planned this," she accused. "You let Sybil think we were…*involved.*" She could barely get that last word out. "You sent the flowers to make it seem as if Sybil's story held water."

"Not only did I let Sybil think we were involved," he replied, "I told her we were."

"What?" she squeaked. That was the best she could manage without drawing attention. Inside, however, she felt like screaming.

"Right after you left last night, I had an unexpected run-in with Sybil. Apparently she witnessed enough to know we'd been arguing."

Kayla closed her eyes. It was a nightmare, a complete nightmare.

"I'll say this for her," Noah continued, "that woman has a nose for gossip like a bloodhound on a scent." He regarded her blandly. "Anyway, I made some sarcastic remark about a lovers' spat, and she took it seriously. I was going to correct her when I realized it would be much more fun to make the most of the situation."

"So instead of letting her believe we were arguing, you told her that we were *involved?*" she asked incredulously.

"What's the matter?" he asked. "Uncomfortable being the subject of rumors? Not too pleasant, is it?"

"You're enjoying this, aren't you?"

He shrugged. "I'll admit to some grim satisfaction at being handed an opportunity to even the score."

She grabbed her shoulder bag and her blazer. "Let's discuss this somewhere else."

He looked mildly surprised. "If you say so."

They had to talk, she thought, but this wasn't the place to do it. She wasn't about to provide fodder for the office gossip mill. But somehow she had to convince him to call Sybil and get her to print a retraction. The alternative didn't bear thinking about. She refused to be lumped together with Huffy, Fluffy and Buffy.

As he followed her down the hall and into an elevator, she was aware of his tread behind her—and of the glances that the two of them attracted.

When they got downstairs and outside into the still-warm September sun, she sighed with relief. At least they were away from prying eyes.

Turning to Noah, her brows snapping together, she began, "Now look—"

Her planned reprimand ended with a gasp as he swept her into his arms.

Her eyes widened. "What—"

Out of the corner of her eye, she saw a man—a photographer—leap forward and snap a shot of them just before Noah's mouth closed over hers.

Two

Kayla put her hands on Noah's chest and pushed, but he held firm.

For the next few seconds, several thoughts tumbled through her mind. Who was that guy with the camera? Were any of her co-workers around? She'd be mortified! What the heck was wrong with Noah? However, those thoughts were quickly drowned out by one overwhelming sensation: the feel of Noah's lips on hers.

He kissed expertly: his lips soft but sure and his focus concentrated on making her *feel*. His big, solid body pressed against her. He smelled of soap and shaving cream and just plain *guy*, and tasted of mint and warmth and subtle sweetness. He overloaded all her senses at once, and she was intoxicated.

It was like being kissed by the captain of the football team in front of the entire school—except she was a twenty-seven-year-old woman with a job and rent payments who happened to be standing in front of her office building at exactly the time that her boss or innumerable other people might be happening by.

That last thought brought her back to reality with a *thunk!*

She pulled her mouth from Noah's and shoved him away.

Noah loosened his hold on her—the expression on his face a mixture of pleasant surprise and—*help*—male curiosity.

"What are you doing?" she demanded, then glanced around. The guy with the camera was still there, snapping away. "And, you! Who are you?"

When he lowered his camera, she recognized him as a photographer for the *Boston World.*

Suddenly she felt ill.

The photographer, who frequently worked with Sybil LaBreck, smiled and waved at her. "Hey, there, Kayla. You know, if I hadn't just seen it with my own eyes, I'd never have believed the rumor about you and Noah." He shook his head bemusedly.

She didn't have a chance to respond because just then she noticed that, striding down the sidewalk toward them, on his way to the office, was Ed O'Neill, managing editor of the *Sentinel.*

Her boss.

She whirled back to Noah.

One look at his amused face, however, and she realized she hadn't just been sunk, she'd been torpedoed—or, more precisely, set up.

The irony wasn't lost on her either: she'd just been photographed apparently kissing *him* in the same way *he'd* been snapped apparently kissing Fluffy.

She jabbed a finger into his chest. "You! This was all part of the plan, wasn't it?"

Noah caught her finger. "Sweetie—" he said, and she knew he was playing to the audience "—is it really so bad to announce our love to the world?"

She yanked her hand away from his.

"Hello, Kayla."

The two of them turned, and she came face-to-face with Ed, whose expression said he was wondering what the hell was going on.

"Er—hello, Ed." She smiled brightly.

Noah held out his hand. "Hi, Ed."

Noah knew her boss?

Ed took it and said gruffly, "Noah. What brings you here first thing in the morning?"

Noah looked amused. "Well—"

"We were just saying goodbye," Kayla interrupted, then took a step toward the *Sentinel*'s entrance. "I'll take the elevator up with you, Ed."

Ed looked from one to the other of them, then glanced at the photographer at the curb. "Anyone want to explain to me what's going on?"

She was going to die, right there in front of the *Sen-*

tinel's headquarters. She could already see the headline: Ms. Rumor-Has-It Slain by Innuendo.

Noah smiled. "Sorry, Ed. Gotta run." His eyes met hers. "I'm sure Kayla will explain everything. Won't you, honey?"

She gritted her teeth while Ed raised his eyebrows at the endearment. *"Of course,"* she said. "Say hello to Huffy, Fluffy and Buffy for me, won't you?"

His eyes laughed at her. "Sure."

To Ed, she said in a low voice, "There's a *Boston World* photographer standing at the curb. I'll explain, but once we're inside."

At Ed's nod, she turned and stalked toward the revolving doors. Later, she promised herself, she'd take some time to throw darts at Noah Whittaker's picture or burn him in effigy.

The only silver lining to this morning's catastrophe was that, since he'd now exacted his revenge, with any luck she'd never have anything to do with him again.

Unfortunately, luck happened to be vacationing in Tahiti the next day.

"Ed, you can't be serious!"

Why were they discussing having her drive over to Whittaker Enterprises to cover a press conference? A press conference at which Noah Whittaker would be presiding!

Hadn't she explained everything to Ed yesterday? Hadn't she explained that she and Noah really loathed each other? Did she not detail how the "affair" had just been a rumor generated by Noah as payback for the stories she'd printed about his bad behavior?

The fact that panic roiled through her at the thought of facing Noah Whittaker again had nothing to do with yesterday's kiss and everything to do with the fact that she couldn't stand the man. He was altogether too high-and-mighty for her taste.

She regarded Ed levelly. He was her boss but also her mentor—surely he could see that sending her to cover this press conference wasn't the best allocation of personnel.

Ed scratched his balding pate. It was the second time he'd done so since showing up at her cubicle. "Look, I thought you were gunning for a position covering hard news."

"I was! I am!" she exclaimed in dismay. She'd gotten into journalism so she could be a business reporter, not so she could write about the latest fashions at debutante balls.

"Well, here's your chance to prove yourself," Ed said. "Rob was supposed to cover this press conference at eleven o'clock, but he's off on a breaking story and everyone else has a full plate."

"I know, but Noah Whittaker hates me. He'll never field a question from me." Her opportunity to cover hard news wasn't supposed to arrive *like this*.

"So?" Ed countered. "When you get there make nice with Noah, smooth over any ruffled feathers, and everything will be fine."

Kayla wished she could be as confident as Ed that she could make nice. It was more likely she'd wind up conking Noah on the head with her purse: Sybil LaBreck's column that morning featured a picture of her and Noah kissing in front of the *Sentinel*'s offices.

"If you do nothing else, just make sure you pick up a copy of the press release that they give out," Ed said, seeming to take some pity on her. "That'll give you enough to write a where, what, how, and when article about whatever it is that Whittaker is announcing today."

She felt her shoulders slump. "Right."

"Jones," Ed said gruffly, "I've been trying to look out for you since the day you got here. You've got enough ambition to fill a football stadium. Now go and put it to good use."

She should have been grateful for Ed's little pep talk. Instead, all she could do was manage some weak waves of the cheerleading pom-poms. She smiled wanly. "Thanks, Ed."

"And," Ed continued, "if you're interested in getting a position on the business beat, Noah Whittaker is as good a person as any to start with."

"What do you mean?"

Ed shrugged. "I mean there have been rumors circulating for a while about some suspicious offshore company in the Cayman Islands linked to Noah Whittaker. It could be nothing, but you never know. If there's a story there, it would be big because Whittaker has a pristine business reputation." He added significantly, "A story like that could practically guarantee you the job you want."

Kayla didn't have to ask what kind of story Ed meant.

She knew that some offshore companies were just tax havens for the wealthy. Others, however, provided excellent cover for money laundering and other shady dealings simply because some localities required very little information to be made public about the companies created there.

Her mind skittered across the idea of Noah connected to something less than completely legal. What could his motivation be? He had all the money he needed. Yet, wasn't her own biological father proof that greed knew no bounds?

Aloud, she said, "Thanks for the tip."

Ed nodded curtly. "I'm willing to give you a chance." Then he nodded at the clock on the wall. "You better get going."

"Right!" she said with as much enthusiasm as she could muster.

As Ed walked away, she picked up her handbag and grabbed her jacket. Well, what choice did she have? The things she had to do to pay the bills!

Unlike the women Noah dated, and, for that matter, her classmates at the fancy prep school she'd attended, she didn't have a trust fund to fall back on or family connections to milk to get ahead.

Instead, she'd gotten her foot in the door of the journalism world by getting an entry-level job straight out of college with the *Sentinel*. It hadn't mattered too much that the position was with the "Styles" section of the paper; it had been one of the few job offers she'd gotten and the one that paid the best of a rather pathetic lot.

Initially, she'd done a lot of research and fact-checking, with an occasional byline as time went on. She'd written about everything from the latest fashions to museum openings—when she hadn't been acting as a gofer for Leslie, who'd been the *Sentinel*'s resident Ms. Rumor-Has-It.

But then Leslie had run off with her paramour—a fiftyish, thrice-divorced millionaire who'd parted with wife number three to elope with Leslie to Paris—and Kayla had been left holding the bag, albeit a snazzy Versace number in black satin.

Kayla had been summoned to the managing editor's office, which smelled of the Macanudo cigars that Ed O'Neill liked to sneak behind closed doors.

"Jones," Ed had said, "you're up at bat. We need someone fast, and you're perfect—a classy Grace Kelly type with the right prep-school credentials. You'll fit right in covering your old school pals for the gossip pages."

And she had. She'd jumped at the chance to replace Leslie, not the least because Ed had dangled a significant salary raise as inducement. For her that had been enough.

So what if becoming Ms. Rumor-Has-It hadn't been part of her career aspirations? She'd gotten her own column before she'd turned twenty-five *and* she'd stopped worrying about the rent. There'd be time enough, she'd reasoned, for her to segue to the business-news desk.

But that had been three years ago. She'd done her job,

and well. Too well, in some respects. No one was eager
to see her move away from the society page.

But, despite the seeming glamour of her job, she'd
begun to feel restless. There were only so many cana-
pés that a girl could eat before she felt like regurgitat-
ing on Buffy the Man Slayer's Manolo Blahnik heels.

That's why she'd recently started to lobby for an opportunity to cover some real news. Because Ed was
right about one thing: she was ambitious and refused to
be typecast for the rest of her career as perfect for covering fluff. She was determined to go places.

Unfortunately, today the place that she was heading
was Noah Whittaker's front door.

"Well, it's interesting to see how the tide has turned."

Across the boardroom table, Noah gave Allison a
disgruntled look. He'd just finished explaining how his
recent bad press was baseless. "I know you find this
hopelessly amusing, but *try* to contain your glee."

Allison laughed. "Oh, come on, big brother, don't tell
me you don't see the hilarity in it all! Women used to
chase you the way they'd run to a shoe sale. These days,
though, you're more like last year's shoes—still wear-
able, but you're wondering why you ever bought them."

Quentin and Matt chuckled.

Noah sighed in exasperation.

It wasn't often these days that Noah's whole family
was together, but early morning meetings of Whittaker
Enterprises' board of directors afforded them the opportunity from time to time, despite their busy lives.

He looked around the room. They were an impressive bunch, and, though he and his siblings could needle each other mercilessly, they had an unshakable bond.

At the head of the table sat his father, James, who, in his retirement, still chaired the board of directors. His mother, Ava—who'd passed along her coloring of dark brown hair and vivid blue eyes to his brother Matt and his sister Allison—was a respected family court judge. Matt, who was older than Noah by two years, was also a vice president at Whittaker, though he'd increasingly been developing his own business interests. Allison had followed their mother's footsteps into the legal profession and become an assistant district attorney in Boston. Quentin, the oldest sibling, was CEO of Whittaker Enterprises.

Missing were Quentin's wife, Liz, who was at home with their baby, Nicholas, and Allison's husband of one month, Connor Rafferty, who ran his own security business.

Noah supposed, given his siblings' penchant for ribbing each other, he shouldn't have been surprised that, once the board meeting had ended, and because they had time to kill before the press conference at eleven, the topic of conversation would turn to the recent headlines about him in the newspapers.

Thanks to Kayla, in the span of two weeks, he'd been branded a philanderer for fooling around with Fluffy, been reported to have had a public scuffle with Huffy during which she'd slapped him and he'd been seen restraining her and, to top it off, been witnessed having an argument with Ms. Rumor-Has-It herself.

He wondered whether Kayla had seen Sybil LaBreck's column that morning and figured she must have. Sybil's headline screamed: Kayla and Noah Kiss and Make Up!

Fortunately, Huffy—er, Eve, he corrected himself, annoyed that now he was unintentionally adopting Kayla's ridiculous names—was in Europe on a modeling shoot and thus probably unaware of the headlines linking her most recent ex to a secret affair with Ms. Rumor-Has-It. Otherwise, he might have had another irate female to contend with.

In any case, he took grim satisfaction in knowing Sybil's column that day had probably riled Kayla. After all, *he* had to suffer through grief from his family.

"Well," Allison continued, "I, for one, would love to congratulate Kayla Jones." She looked at Quentin and Matt for affirmation. "Unlike those vapid, vampish vixens you sometimes date, she's smart enough not to be bowled over by your charm, Noah."

Noah mouthed *vapid, vampish vixens* incredulously while his brothers stifled their mirth. Then he frowned. "Great. I'll let Connor know that, if you ever get tired of the D.A.'s office, you can have a second career as a gossip columnist." He added, "Does family loyalty mean nothing to you?"

"Not since you tried to get me married off to Connor," Allison returned sweetly. "How did you put it to him?" She pretended to try to remember for a second, then snapped her fingers. "Oh, right. I believe your words were 'Why don't you help take her off our hands?'"

Noah grumbled. "Maybe I shouldn't have put it like that, but you and Connor belonged together. *This* situation's different."

Matt's lips twitched. "Ms. Rumor-Has-It does seem to have your number, unlike—uh, how did she put it?— *Huffy, Fluffy and Buffy.* And, on top of it all, your little columnist is undeniably *hot.*"

Noah quelled the sudden, inexplicable urge to slug the amused look off of his brother's face. So, Kayla was hot; she was also a menace, and she was *not* "his" little columnist. "Yeah, and she's also a consummate teller of tall tales in that fiction column of hers."

At the head of the table, his father cleared his throat and gave him a level look. "The bottom line is there's a problem here that you need to fix. Even if there's not a modicum of truth in the recent headlines, they're bad for public relations—both yours and Whittaker Enterprises'."

Quentin nodded. "Dad's right, as much as I'd like to think otherwise. Some people will believe the press, and even those who don't will wonder if you're playing and partying harder than you're working."

Noah watched his mother cast him a sympathetic look that nonetheless managed to carry a hint of reproach. "I know I raised you to be respectful toward women, Noah, so I have no doubt that the recent press about you is just an aberration. Nevertheless, darling, I have to agree with your father and brother. You must fix this. No more headlines, and you should try to do something to repair your public image."

Noah knew his family was right. His philosophy of

working hard and playing harder had long worked for him, but then Ms. Rumor-Has-It had come along.

He had to deal with her and the trouble she'd stirred up in his life.

What was she doing here?

Noah stared in disbelief at the figure slinking into a seat at the back of the roomful of assembled reporters, cameramen and photographers awaiting the beginning of the press conference.

As if she could go unnoticed.

Even if she hadn't been a head-turner with her blond hair falling like a curtain past her shoulders and a figure that was a siren call to every straight guy in the room, she had on a ridiculous outfit consisting of a pale pink sweater made of some clingy material that hugged her breasts, a pencil-thin pinstriped skirt showing off legs that went on and on, and some *come-hither* heels.

Watching as she got a once-over from the guy next to her while, oblivious to any attention, she pulled out a notepad, Noah smiled grimly: *I rest my case.*

Much to his annoyance, the memory of their kiss lingered with him. Her lips had been soft, silky and full beneath his, and their effect had gone through him like a shot of brandy. But so what if the woman had proved she could kiss with real feeling?

He frowned. The last thing he needed to be thinking about right now was their kiss. The press conference would start any minute. He'd resolved this morning to deal with her, but he hadn't expected to be confronted with an opportunity here, now, surrounded by half the press of Greater Boston. Hell.

Anyway, the real question was, what was she doing here? Last time he'd checked, gossip columnists didn't cover breaking business news.

As the clock on the back wall hit eleven, he strode to the podium at the front of the room. He was going to announce the acquisition by Whittaker Enterprises of Avanti Technologies, a small company located along Route 128, Boston's high-tech corridor, and because the acquisition of Avanti impacted Whittaker's computer business—his area of expertise—he'd be doing the initial presentation. Afterward, he and Quentin, as well as the president of Avanti, would field questions.

When Noah got to the microphone, he made a couple of jokes to break the ice, then consulted his notes: "Pleased to announce...welcome the opportunity to work with...corporate synergies involved..."

Throughout his speech, he noticed Kayla kept her gaze fixed somewhere over his left shoulder. *Uncomfortable, eh?* He wondered again what had brought her here and knew that, as soon as the press conference was over, he was going find out.

Focusing again on the assembled reporters, he concluded by saying that additional copies of Whittaker's press release were on a table at the back of the room.

Then, when Quentin and the president of Avanti stepped forward to flank him at the mike, he fielded questions from reporters, eventually calling on a guy in jeans.

The reporter stood up, a smirk hovering at the corners of his lips. "The stock for Whittaker Computing has been down recently. Can you comment on the markets' reaction to the recent bad press about you?"

Noah tensed. Whittaker Computing—one of a handful of companies that made up Whittaker Enterprises—was partly publicly owned. There were any number of reasons why Whittaker Computing's stock had taken a hit recently, as any half-wit could tell you, but the weasel in front of him was obviously trying to bait him.

Noah gave him a semblance of a smile and then, keeping his tone even, said, "The markets have better things to do than follow any spurious rumors written about me."

Noah watched as Kayla slunk farther down in her chair at the back of the room. Feeling a tad self-conscious, was she? *Well, welcome to the club, babe.*

He started to call on another questioner, but the smirking jerk in jeans—probably some overeager new recruit looking to make his mark—persisted. "What about the impression you've given that you can't get along with women? There's been speculation that this could affect Whittaker's ability to recruit female executives."

Noah gripped the sides of the lectern. He'd like to deck the questioning little dweeb. "Maybe it's a question of the ability of a few particular women to get along with me."

This earned him a chuckle or two from the audience.

He held the reporter's gaze until the guy shifted. "Whittaker Enterprises is an equal opportunity employer. We value and welcome female employees. In fact, we're proud we've been rated one of the best places for women to work by a leading Boston magazine. Our on-site day care and flextime schedules are models for the industry. The women at Whittaker who work with me wouldn't tell you differently."

Then, determined this time to cut off the smart-ass, Noah turned to look at another part of the room. "Next question."

Fifteen minutes later, the press conference was over. Immediately, he spotted Kayla scurrying into the hall.

"Excuse me," he said curtly, shoving his way past the milling press and striding out of the room.

He caught up with her halfway down the hall and captured her elbow. "We need to talk."

She started and looked up at him guiltily.

"What?" he asked blandly. "Attempting to make your escape?"

"I'm sure we've said all there is to say to one another," she said, her tone cool enough to freeze penguins in their tracks.

"On the contrary, Barbie," he countered dryly, looking pointedly at her blond hair and pink sweater.

She pulled her elbow away from him. "I'm not going anywhere with you. I may be Barbie, but you're no Ken, Mr. I-Change-Women-with-the-Seasons Whittaker. Barbie and Ken had a committed, monogamous relationship for over forty years."

God, she was maddening. She'd just compared him *unfavorably* to a plastic doll's main squeeze.

He wondered again why he still found her pulse-poundingly attractive. Sick. He was sick.

"As unpleasant as it is for the both of us, we need to talk and I suggest we do it in private—unless you want our public bloodletting to continue?" He took her elbow again.

She looked around. "I'll scream."

Aside from the two of them, no one was in the hallway yet. They were some distance from the room where the press conference had been held, and probably most of the journalists were still gathering their equipment. Still, Noah knew that Kayla could make herself heard.

"I wouldn't advise it," he said dryly. "Not unless you want another newspaper headline about us, and I doubt that."

She opened her mouth.

"Think about it," he said forcefully. "Our names conjoined in ink. Again. *Forever.*"

Three

Upstairs in Noah's office, Kayla still couldn't shake the feeling that this was a bad idea. A very bad idea.

They didn't do well talking to each other. Or even being in the same room together.

Noah gestured her to a seat.

"No thanks," she said.

"Suit yourself," he responded, then sat at the edge of his desk, folding his arms across his chest and crossing one foot over the other at the ankle.

She glanced around his office. It was all chrome and black and glass with two walls displaying great views of nearby hills. Her cubicle at work would have fit into the space behind his desk.

Grudgingly, she admitted that, whatever else Noah was, he did appear to be spectacularly successful.

"What the heck are you doing here?" he asked abruptly, drawing her attention back to him.

"I was filling in for another reporter," she said, self-conscious under his scrutiny. All at once, her skirt felt too short, her top too tight and her heels too high. Damn him.

He raised a brow. "Since when are gossip columnists asked to fill in for business reporters?"

It was on the tip of her tongue to tell him that it was none of his business, when it occurred to her that she'd just been handed a great chance to ask as many questions as she wanted about the acquisition of Avanti—*if*, that was, she acted at least passably civil toward him.

"I've been trying for a lateral move to the business desk at the *Sentinel*," she responded stiffly.

She could see she'd surprised him. "You want to write something other than salacious rumors?"

She checked her temper. "Let's not cross that ground again, shall we? As I think I made clear before, I work hard at my job. It's just that I want to be doing the type of reporting that I got into journalism for."

"And that would be—?"

"Business reporting," she said, her tone clipped. "Are you going to tell me what you wanted to talk to me about, or not?"

He looked at her for several seconds, his green gaze inscrutable. Finally, he said, "I'm calling for a cease-fire."

"What?" It was her turn to be taken by surprise.

"You heard me."

"Oh, right. I suppose now that the empire has struck back, it's okay for *you* to want to call a truce. After all, Sybil LaBreck has just announced *to the whole world* that we're back together!"

"Yeah, well," he said, too placidly to suit her, "you did play straight into my hands on that one."

She stared at him, annoyed. How dare he stand there looking so sexy and so gorgeous—causing an unwanted but very feminine reaction in her—when he was such a calculating sneak. She folded her arms across her chest. "I know I will regret asking, but how did I play into your plans?"

"Yesterday I tipped off that photographer from the *Boston World* so he could snap me leaving the *Sentinel*'s offices looking, uh, contrite after trying to mend fences with you."

"I should have guessed that photographer wasn't just hanging around hoping for a good photo op."

"Little did I know you'd insist on walking out with me—"

"Giving you and him an even better photo opportunity than you were expecting," she finished for him.

The lout.

"So, again, are you willing to declare a truce?"

"What kind of truce?" she asked, suspicious.

He shrugged nonchalantly, rising from his desk.

She forced herself not to take an involuntary step back just to keep some space between them. Over six feet, he had a comfortable height advantage over her—

even when she was wearing heels. But, more than that, he radiated a charisma that was nearly palpable.

"We can help each other."

"Really?" she asked in disbelief, forcing herself to keep up with their war of words because it was easier than thinking about being alone in his office with him. "I can't imagine what help I need from you other than for you to stop sabotaging me."

He arched a brow. "*Sabotage* is a strong word, don't you think?"

"Not if it's accurate." When he was smooth and charming, he was even more dangerous than when he was angry and annoyed. She brushed aside the disgruntling realization.

"You just said you're looking to move to the business desk at the *Sentinel.*"

"Yes...?" She wondered where he was going with this.

"I can give you a news story that will help you get there."

"What news story?"

"An exclusive inside look at Whittaker Enterprises. I'll grant you broad access."

"In return for...?"

He gazed at her speculatively. "In return for your help in rehabilitating my public image."

"Impossible," she responded.

He laughed. "I'm flattered, in a backhanded-compliment sort of way."

"Anyway, you're overestimating my influence on public opinion."

"I don't think so. You damaged my reputation, you can repair it."

"How?"

"By being seen getting along with me."

"I'm not that good of an actress," she retorted.

"Do your best. I'm not looking for an Oscar-winning performance."

His plan was ridiculous, outrageous. So why was she tempted?

Because, she answered herself, he was dangling an irresistible lure, damn him. She'd walk on hot coals to get that business reporter's beat.

"Well?" he prompted.

"Can't. Journalistic ethics. You may have heard of them."

"A little late in the day to be worrying about those, don't you think?" he scoffed.

"Tell that to my boss when he fires me," she snapped.

He shrugged and folded his arms again. "What would it take not to offend your journalistic sensibilities?"

"I won't agree to anything that smacks of you trying to buy me off or of an exchange of favors."

He sighed. "I told you that you'll have broad access to Whittaker Enterprises. You can talk to our employees. Heck, *I'll* talk to you. You can follow me around and see what my routine is. I won't stop you from writing something unflattering. All I'm asking for is that you write a balanced piece."

She continued to eye him, unconvinced.

He sighed again. "Fine, you don't have to pretend to

get along with me anymore than comes naturally, if that's going to trouble your reporter's conscience."

"Thanks."

"And as far as Ms. Rumor-Has-It's column goes, I think you can use the story about Whittaker Enterprises to your advantage. Just tell Ed that you can't write about me in your regular column while you're pursuing an in-depth piece about Whittaker Enterprises because you want to avoid any conflicts. If he's worried, he can assign you an intern. That way, when you do get moved over to the business desk, you'll already have someone in place to take over as Ms. Rumor-Has-It."

He made his plan sound so reasonable—and appealing. Oh-so-appealing. Nevertheless, she had to ask, "What about Sybil?"

He looked untroubled. "What about her? I'll call her up and explain our affair was a hoax. Besides, as long as we spread the word that you're shadowing me in order to write a piece about Whittaker Enterprises, we'll be dispelling the rumor that we're involved."

The thought of Sybil having the rug pulled out from under her *did* make his plan more tempting. Kayla bit her lip, then said, "What's in this for you?"

"For my part, I'm banking your intern won't be as interested in my social life as you are." He gave her a sardonic look. "Besides, since—thanks to you—I'm currently free of models and actresses, there won't be anything exciting to write about."

"Maybe." She refused to concede he likely was right.

"On top of that," he said, warming to his subject,

"once you get your assignment to the business desk at the *Sentinel,* I'm rid of you—at least as a wrecking ball in my social life. And, as an added bonus, I get a balanced news piece about Whittaker Enterprises." He finished triumphantly, "The plan is perfect."

She considered him a moment. "What would be the terms?" she asked, hoping she wouldn't regret this, yet unable to pass up the opportunity he presented.

She saw the flare of gratification in his eyes, but he quickly banked it. "Terms?"

"Yes. I need to know you'll give me access to information soon and won't renege on me." Now that she'd let herself entertain his offer, she wasn't going to be shy about the particulars.

He arched a brow. "Suspicious, aren't you?"

"There has to be a time limit," she said firmly.

"Make your best offer," he countered.

She assessed him, then took a moment to ponder. No doubt he was a shrewd bargainer—after all, he'd just engineered the takeover of one of Boston's leading tech firms by Whittaker Enterprises. "Two weeks."

He shook his head. "Six."

"Three." Nearly a month was fair.

"Five," he said. "These things take time."

"Let's split the difference," she countered. "Four. It shouldn't take long to repair the damage."

"A pleasure doing business with you." He closed the space between them and held out his hand.

Relief, followed by panic, washed through her. *What*

have I just done? She took his hand, felt her own engulfed in his, and experienced a surge of sensation.

Judging by the look in his eye, he felt it, too.

She started to draw away, but he pulled her closer.

He lifted her chin with his free hand and she had just a moment to lower her eyelids before he brushed her lips with his.

The kiss was over in the space of a few heartbeats, but its impression—powerful and disturbing—lingered for her.

He drew back and gazed down at her, his expression inscrutable. "Just checking," he murmured.

"What?" She looked at him, eyes wide, as she strove to clear her brain.

He smiled wryly. "You didn't need to worry about whether your acting abilities were up to the challenge." At her displeased expression, he laughed. "I know, I know. I'm diabolical."

Kayla was grateful he couldn't read her mind—for while *diabolical* should have been the first word that popped into her head, disturbingly, instead, it had been *delicious*.

How does one dress for dinner with a couple of computer geeks from Silicon Valley? Kayla wondered.

The day after the press conference, Noah had phoned her to announce that, if she was going to be shadowing him for purposes of her article, she should attend a business dinner that he had scheduled on Friday night with a couple of young hotshots from the West Coast.

He'd also let her know that, in the meantime, he'd
done as promised and called Sybil to say his supposed
relationship with Ms. Rumor-Has-It had been a hoax
that he'd perpetuated to get even. Ironically, Sybil had
been reluctant to believe there *wasn't* a relationship.
Perhaps hedging her bets, however, her headline in the
next morning's paper had read: Noah Denies Relationship with Ms. Rumor-Has-It.

Kayla figured she'd take what she could get and
Sybil's headline was better than nothing. Eventually, the
story about her and Noah *would* fade away.

And the good news was she'd been able to convince
Ed to do what Noah had suggested. Ed had been pleased
Noah had agreed to cooperate on an in-depth profile of
Whittaker Enterprises. More importantly, he'd also grudgingly agreed to give her sometime assistant, Jody Donaldson, who was just a year out of college, a greater role
in the writing of the Ms. Rumor-Has-It column, including writing anything newsworthy about Noah Whittaker.

So far, Kayla admitted to herself, everything was
going according to plan—*if* she could figure out what
to wear to this dinner tonight.

She began looking through her closet again from one
end to the other. She tossed aside the leather miniskirt
that she'd recently worn to the Avalon, one of Boston's
well-known nightclubs.

Dress down, Noah had said. Though tonight technically counted as business, Noah had advised her that the
term *business* had a whole different meaning among the
under-thirty-five, newly rich and geeky set created by

the information-technology boom, particularly in Silicon Valley.

She didn't doubt what he had told her. Sure, she herself had been part of the business-casual-attire revolution that had swept corporate offices across the United States in the past ten years. But, as a society columnist, she knew the requirements for her were different from those for some of her contemporaries: she was more high fashion and less grunge fashion. She was expected to blend with the social set she covered and, since she didn't have a trust fund or even a salary that was anything to brag about, she spent a good deal of time haunting outlet stores and consignment shops.

This all, of course, left her lost as far as what tonight required. Exasperated, she kept moving through the hangers in her closet, fretfully passing on her Levi's 501 blue jeans. *I have nothing to wear!* she silently wailed in frustration.

The phone rang and she felt a stab of relief at the unexpected distraction, despite the fact that she had only about an hour left before Noah would pick her up.

"Hello," she said absently, her eyes skimming the disarrayed pile of clothes on her bed.

"You sound as perky as usual," a voice said dryly.

"Samantha?"

Despite being seven years apart, Kayla and her sister shared a close bond, perhaps because they had no other siblings. Technically, they were half siblings, though she never thought of the two of them that way. When Kayla was five, her mother had remarried, and

Greg Jones had adopted Kayla. She had been happy to have a father in her life and even happier when, two years later, a baby sister had arrived. From the beginning, Samantha had followed in Kayla's footsteps, right up to enrolling at Tufts University, Kayla's alma mater.

The pile of clothes forgotten, she asked, "Is something wrong? Did something happen?"

Samantha laughed. "Relax. You sound as bad as Mom. Maybe I just called to say hello."

"Not if you're twenty and a college junior and it's a Friday night," she countered.

"Welcome to my lackluster social life. I'm hoping things will turn around soon," her sister responded. "Why am I not surprised *you're* at home tonight?"

"Actually, I need to leave in an hour."

"Oh?" Her sister's tone brightened. "Hot date?"

"Not really."

"Come on, spill the goods. Who's the guy?"

Kayla hesitated for a second, then resigned herself to the inevitable. "Noah Whittaker."

Silence reigned on the other end of the phone line.

"Samantha?"

"I'm speechless."

"That would be a first."

"Noah Whittaker is hot, hot, hot." Her sister sighed dreamily. "You've come to your senses. Though, if you've finally decided to date guys who are hunk-a-licious, I'm surprised it's Noah. You've been lacerating him in your column."

"Right, and speaking of which…" With one eye on

the clock, she brought her sister up to speed on her agreement with Noah, ending with, "So, what should I wear?"

"What should you wear?" Samantha said laughingly.
"Is that all you can say?"

Frowning, she said, "Well, what should I say?"

"How about, this is an opportunity most women
would die for! How about, it's not every day a sinfully
delicious millionaire asks me to dinner? How about,
how can I get Noah Whittaker to carry me off to his
lovely penthouse in the sky?"

"How about, get your head out of the clouds?" Kayla
countered. "Besides, this is strictly business."

"Oh, Kayla, live a little! Besides, there's no telling
where things could go *after* you get your story." Samantha dropped her voice. "Laugh with the sinners for once."

"Coming from my little sister, I find that comment
somewhat distressing," Kayla said with mock severity.
"But for the record, Noah Whittaker doesn't just prefer
to laugh with the sinners. He likes to party with the
devil."

"Okay, whatever. Have it your way," Samantha said in
exasperation. "Now, let's see…. I know! What about the
camisole top that you got at a Filene's sale? Very sexy."

"Too sexy," Kayla said emphatically, thinking of the
silky top's spaghetti straps and lace-edged cups. "It's
practically lingerie."

"Exactly."

Kayla glanced at the clock again. She was running
out of time and getting desperate. If she paired the camisole with some black pants, heels and a wrap, she *would*

have an evening look that was dressy but casual, not to mention sexy and cool. She bit her lip.

"Go for it, Kayla," Samantha said, evidently sensing her hesitancy.

She sighed. "You know, you still haven't told me why you called."

Her sister laughed. "I'm not pregnant, homeless or desperate for cash. That's all you need to know. And, really, sometimes I am just calling to talk. I'll call you tomorrow to find out how your date went, and you can hear me gush about my *exciting* evening watching old flicks in the dorm's recreation room. Now, go!"

Half an hour later, Kayla found herself opening her front door dressed in black pants and a silky blue camisole top edged with brown lace, her toes peeking out from high-heeled slingbacks. She'd applied some light makeup and left her straight blond hair loose about her shoulders. Her watch and chandelier earrings were her only adornments.

Noah's eyes widened when he saw her, his gaze raking her from head to toe. He looked ready to devour her on the spot.

A shiver ran through her that had nothing to do with being cold. He looked devastatingly attractive in a blazer and a dark gray T-shirt paired with hip-hugging jeans, a five-o'clock shadow darkening his jaw.

"You look great."

She glanced down at her clothes, pleased he approved. "I wasn't sure what you meant when you said tonight was casual."

He tapped a finger on his chest. "*This* is what I meant."

As his blazer gaped open, she noticed the writing printed in black across the top of his T-shirt: Plays Well with Others.

"Geekdom values nonconformity over social acceptance. It's the pursuit of neophilia in its purest form."

At her confused look, he explained, "Neophilia means being excited by novelty. Geeks are big on novelty."

"Oh." Her brow furrowed. "In that case, I'm *not* dressed right."

A smile hovered at the corners of his lips. "No, you're dressed just right. At the risk of sounding sexist, the dress code doesn't apply to women because even computer geeks want to be seen with a babe on their arm. It all goes back to the high-school fantasy of dating the most popular girl in the class."

"That *is* sexist." But he thought she was a babe? She quelled the flutter that gave her.

He nodded, still standing in the doorway.

Inviting him in was too dangerous, and they were running just on time as it was. She held up her hands, one of which clutched a small handbag and a light shawl. "I'm ready when you are."

As she brushed past him, she ignored the grin that spread across his face, one that was all blatant male appreciation and said *ready for what?* Fortunately, he resisted the urge to give voice to what she could read on his face.

When they got downstairs, her attention was drawn to the sleek black Jaguar parked at the curb.

"Welcome to the Batmobile," Noah said with a grin, opening the passenger door for her.

When he'd gone around the car and gotten behind the wheel, she glanced around the luxurious interior and asked, "Why do I suspect that the doors lock, the windows fog up and the passenger-side seat drops back at the driver's command?"

As he turned the ignition, he tossed her a wicked grin. "I refuse to incriminate myself."

Four

When they arrived at Ginza, a trendy Japanese restaurant, Noah introduced her to the two "executives" from Silicon Valley as a news reporter who was shadowing him for a profile on Whittaker Enterprises.

Tim and Ben, who looked no older than twenty-five, had attended the prestigious California Institute of Technology together. Neither was geeky in the obvious glasses-and-pocket-protector way, but Tim was wearing an orange T-shirt paired with a dark-red blazer, and Ben had used a safety pin to replace a missing button on his shirt.

Kayla discovered they had spent three years toiling away in the bowels of established high-tech companies, working eighty-hour weeks, before they'd decided to strike out on their own—so they could still work eighty-hour weeks but be their own bosses.

Over dinner, the conversation moved across a variety of topics, from which tech company had recently lured a top employee from a rival to which new computer software products would soon be launched onto the market. To her disappointment, however, there were no hints as to what sort of business relationship, if any, Noah was contemplating with Tim and Ben's company.

However, if tonight was any indication, it didn't seem as if Noah would have any reason to be interested in nefarious offshore investments in the Cayman Islands or elsewhere. He had enough people with legitimate businesses knocking on his door.

Soon, the conversation at dinner veered to her job at the *Sentinel.* Both Ben and Tim were fascinated by her position as Ms. Rumor-Has-It, which they viewed as glamorous.

It made her want to laugh. She earned a fraction of what they made—and what they could make in the future. She wondered how glamorous they'd think her life was if they saw the small apartment she lived in and the car she'd been driving since her high-school days.

Noah, she noticed, didn't say anything. Not even a peep about being a favorite target for her column. That was, until Tim asked how she chose her stories. "Yes, Kayla," Noah interjected in a bland voice, "how *do* you choose your stories?"

She ignored him, keeping her attention instead on

Tim and Ben, who seemed unaware that Noah was one of her favorite targets. "I try to write stories that people want to read." She shrugged. "But I suppose personal taste comes into play in deciding whether the focus is going to be on politicians, celebrities or other figures."

"So what do you focus on?" Ben asked.

"I look for stories that are humorous—it's always amusing to poke fun at egos and pretensions."

Next to her, Noah guffawed and shifted in his chair, his leg brushing hers.

She tensed but forced herself to keep looking at Tim and Ben. "Of course, sometimes I don't have to look. The stories come to me."

"People want to appear in your column?" Tim asked curiously.

"You'd be surprised. There's a love-hate relationship between journalists and celebrities' publicists or press agents. Sometimes handlers want publicity in order to keep their celebrity in the public eye. But if a celebrity gets caught in a scandal-worthy situation, his publicist will be on the phone faster than you can say 'libel suit' to try to get you not to print the story. That is, if they don't have a hope of convincingly denying the truth of the story outright."

Tim laughed, and Ben said, "Marvelous!"

"How do you get the dirt on your victims to begin with?" Noah asked.

She turned to look at him fully. Mild annoyance was stamped on his face. "Now that would be telling, wouldn't it?"

"I thought *telling* was what you did for a living," he retorted.

She could come up with an appropriate rejoinder to that, but, she reminded herself, she had to do a passable job of getting along with Noah. At least until she got this story. Then all bets were off.

She smiled brightly at the younger guys facing her. "Just about anyone can be a source. Doormen, bouncers, waiters. Sometimes rivals or so-called friends call in tips, and then, of course, there are the anonymous tipsters."

"Have you gotten any good tips from anonymous sources?" Ben asked.

"Yup." She took a sip from her glass of sake. "I've broken a few stories because of them, too."

Ben raised his eyebrows, and Tim said, "Wow."

"The last story I broke was about the CEO of a troubled department-store chain—"

"I remember when he hit the papers," Noah interjected.

She nodded. "It turned out he was buying five-thousand-dollar shower mats for his penthouse while his shareholders were bleeding money."

"Ouch," Tim said.

"What happened?" Ben asked.

"He's no longer CEO," Noah said, answering for her. "Just like, if Kayla has her way, I'll no longer be the playboy of the northern hemisphere."

Tim stifled a smile, while Ben looked from her to Noah and back.

Kayla groaned inwardly. Great. Tim and Ben obviously thought something was going on between her and Noah.

After dinner, they headed to a karaoke bar. Though going to a bar where the patrons were encouraged to stand up and sing popular tunes wasn't her thing, she was soon laughing and clapping along with everyone else as one guest after another tried to carry a tune, assisted by a microphone, a DJ who loaded the right soundtrack and a TV monitor that displayed the song's lyrics.

The dim lighting in the bar, as well as the intimacy of their seating arrangement at a small table, kept Kayla acutely aware of Noah, who was seated next to her.

So intent was she on the accidental brush of his leg against hers that she was startled when Noah spoke. "So what's it going to be?"

"What?" she asked uncomprehendingly.

He indicated the small stage with a quirk of an eyebrow. "What are you going to sing?"

"*No,*" she said, shaking her head.

"Chicken," he teased.

She straightened her spine. "I haven't sung since I was in the junior-high-school chorus."

"Not even in the shower?"

"That's not in public."

"So you do sing in the shower?" he asked. "Funny, I didn't think you were the singing-in-the-shower type."

"And you are?" she parried.

"I've done many things in the shower," he said, his look wicked. "Singing is just one of them."

"The question is, are you good at any of them?"

Noah threw back his head and laughed, drawing the momentary attention of Ben and Tim, who were seated in front of them, closer to the stage, watching someone do a torturous rendition of "Midnight Train to Georgia."

Kayla felt Noah's laugh to the tips of her toes. It was low, rich and seductive.

"Come on," he said. "I'll get up there if you will. It's practically required. Even Ben and Tim are taking a turn."

As it turned out, Ben and Tim did a passable rap duet.

She was sort of stunned actually, but all Noah said was "Like I said, the name of the game is novelty."

"Where do they find the time with their work schedules?"

Noah shrugged. "Rapping helps them attract women."

Her turn came a few minutes later. She walked to the stage and, in a snap decision, told the DJ to change her song selection.

If the name of the game was doing something out of character, she knew how to oblige.

As the first notes of the song vibrated through the room, she closed her eyes for a few seconds and let herself get caught up in the mood.

Finally, she opened her eyes and began singing "Come Away with Me." Norah Jones's hit song was slow, romantic and suited to her own husky singing voice.

For the first minute or so, she avoided looking at Noah. When she did chance a glance at him, her eyes locked with his and she almost stumbled over a note.

At that moment, the strangest set of feelings passed over her. She felt the exhilaration of racing with the wind in her hair alternating with the languor of lying in a hammock on a hot, sunny afternoon. The sensations thrilled and warmed her at the same time.

She sang on about walking together on a cloudy day and a love that would never stop.

Noah's gaze flickered, though the rest of his face appeared etched in cement, and sexual awareness wrapped itself around her like a blanket.

When she was done, her eyes lingered on his. He gazed at her intensely, as if he was stopping himself from bounding onto the stage, sweeping her up and making a beeline for the door.

The thought gave her goose bumps and she told herself to stop being ridiculous. She replaced the microphone on its holder and headed back to their table.

Noah met her in the middle of the room as he made his way to the stage. "Impressive," he murmured. "You should do more than sing in the shower."

"Th-thanks."

When she'd taken her seat again, the DJ began Noah's selection. She recognized the song within a few notes and tensed.

He wouldn't.

But he did.

She felt hot all over as Noah began singing Billy Paul's "Me and Mrs. Jones." Tim and Ben turned around to toss her amused looks, but her gaze was caught and held by Noah's.

As Noah sang about how he and Ms. Jones had a thing going on even though they knew it was wrong, she resisted the urge to fan herself. He had changed the lyrics to "Ms." instead of "Mrs." and she was in danger of dissolving into a puddle under the table.

She lowered her lashes and tried to look around the room. She hoped no one here knew either of them, because he was practically inviting headlines in tomorrow's paper!

Her gaze moved back to his. The look on his face matched his voice: smoky and full of sensual promise.

Oh, God.

Kayla wasn't sure how she lasted through Noah's song, but, helped by a few fortifying sips of a martini, she did.

When the song ended, Noah grinned, breaking the spell, and then thanked the DJ. As he made his way back to their table, several of the women in the room cast him inviting looks.

Well, she concluded glumly, Noah had proven he *was* good at one thing in the shower. She couldn't prevent herself from thinking about what else he was good at.

Bed. That was Noah's first thought. The second was: he had to ditch his Silicon Valley sidekicks.

As he approached their table, he noticed Kayla appeared flushed and flustered. She seemed to look everywhere but at him.

The air was so sexually charged between them that he was almost afraid to touch her. As it was, he gave them two-to-one odds of winding up in an empty cloak-room, tearing each other's clothes off.

He'd chosen "Me and Mrs. Jones" on a whim, think-ing he'd have some fun with her. But along the way, while he'd been singing about hopes being built up too high, the mood had turned from playful to hot and intense.

He couldn't remember the last time he'd had a con-nection that strong and fast with a woman. The realiza-tion left him bemused.

As he neared, Ben turned to Tim and cracked, "And he can sing, too."

Tim looked up and shrugged, a wry look on his face. "Okay, dude, the T-shirt, the Billy Paul imitation...I guess I've gotta concede."

Noah noticed Kayla continued to remain silent, sip-ping her drink. To Tim and Ben, he said easily, "If I couldn't top you guys on my home turf, I'd have to toss in the towel." He withdrew some bills from his wallet and threw them down on the table. "Since we've got a victor, let's call it a night."

While Ben and Tim thanked him for picking up the tab, Noah cast a covert look at Kayla. She seemed to be getting her bearings.

"You okay?" he asked.

For the first time, she looked directly at him. A range of emotions flickered across her face before she seemed to school it into a polite smile. "Yes, of course."

He moved back so she could precede him to the door. A part of him couldn't wait to get rid of Ben and Tim. The other part warned him that being alone with Kayla right now was not a good idea. He was supposed to be giving her a story. Instead, he was thinking about the shortest route to the bedroom.

He didn't have time to dwell on his thoughts, however, because when they got to the front of the bar, Tim suddenly turned and motioned Noah over. "Bad news," Tim said. "The valet mentioned that a paparazzo with a camera has been spotted outside. The staff here have been telling everyone who's leaving in case they're the reason the guy is here."

Noah muttered a curse under his breath.

Next to him, Kayla tensed.

"Friend of yours?" he asked.

"Don't be ridiculous," she retorted. "Besides, if there's anyone who has a history of siccing journalists on the two of us, it's you."

"Just checking."

"Anyway," she added, "we don't know it's us that he's waiting for. This street has lots of trendy places. He could just be on a fishing expedition, hoping he'll get lucky and snap someone good."

Noah pulled his car keys from his pocket. "Maybe," he said, because he thought she was engaging in wishful thinking, "but the fact is he's out there now, and he may spot us when we walk out of here." Catching the panicked look on her face, he asked, "What's the matter?"

"We can't be photographed together! At least not yet, and definitely not leaving a bar and driving off alone together! Not so soon after Sybil published your denial of a relationship between us. It will undermine everything."

"Ah," he said, because he understood her predicament, having been there one too many times himself. "Welcome to my world, baby doll."

"We can't go out there!" she reiterated.

"Throwing yourself on my mercy, are you?" he said, then added, relenting, "Fine. We'll make the most of the fact that he may not know we're in here." He looked toward the rear of the bar. "There should be a fire exit at the back."

"What—?" As comprehension dawned, she shook her head. "Oh, no."

"Don't worry," he said, then pretended to grin lecherously. "If there are any walls to scale, I'll give you a boost—unless you have a better idea?"

She sighed.

"Great." He shook hands with Tim and Ben. "Gentlemen, I believe this is where we part company. Kayla and I are going to use the back exit to make our getaway. I doubt our cameraman is after either of you, but your leaving will provide a distraction in case Kayla and I need one."

Tim and Ben nodded, and Tim joked to Ben, "Have you noticed he always gets the girl at the end, too?"

Noah chuckled and said, "Not always."

Kayla rolled her eyes. "Infamous on the West Coast as well, hmm?"

He winked at her because he knew it would irritate her, and he wasn't disappointed.

They left Tim and Ben then and, with the help of the bar manager, made their way to the back of the bar and out the fire exit.

As it turned out, they didn't have to worry about scaling walls. There was an alley that ended at a side street. From there, they walked to where Noah's car was parked.

Once they'd hit the road, Noah said wryly, "Tonight was the sort of thing that passes as business entertainment among the wonder boys of high-tech. Just be glad there wasn't a *Star Trek* convention in town."

"Tim and Ben are nice guys."

Her comment amused him. "And I'm not?"

"You're grist for the rumor mill."

He laughed, then sobered. "When your life is fodder for the tabloids, you become familiar with back exits."

When she made no response, he changed the subject. "Seems like you have an interesting job. Makes me wonder why you want to trade it for a hard news beat."

The look she gave him said she hadn't expected him to admit her job had any redeeming qualities. "My job has its moments, but my column is mostly news about local figures because the *Sentinel* doesn't have a hope of competing with national tabloids and magazines."

He flashed her a look. "I figured ambition had to have a place here somewhere. So why don't you apply for a job at one of the national tabloids?"

She didn't answer for a minute, as if weighing what she wanted to reveal. "I'm ready for something besides gossip," she said finally. "Believe it or not, it's tiring to report on Buffy the Man Slayer's latest conquest. And, reporting on celebrities' bad behavior also requires a thick skin."

"How so?"

She slanted him a sideways look. "When you print things that upset people, there's sometimes fallout. And, besides, I don't take pleasure in printing stuff that winds up hurting someone."

Her admission surprised him. In fact, the entire discussion this evening about her job had surprised him. While he was still angry about his own appearances in her column, he was willing to concede he might have been too judgmental in characterizing what she did for a living as telling lies.

While he still wasn't sure whether her column could be thought of as social satire, he could concede there were some areas of his social life—and, God knew, of those of the women he dated—that could easily be mocked.

Yet, he was glad she'd gotten an unexpected taste tonight of dodging paparazzi. He'd seen the worry in her eyes and had felt a modicum of satisfaction in knowing she was stressed over the possibility of being caught with him and of having to stomp out the inevitable flames in the media.

When they got to her apartment complex, he parked and helped her out, then walked with her to the front door of her building, which had a security camera but no doorman.

She took out her keys, then looked up at him. "I'm not sure what to say under the circumstances, but thanks, I had a good time. It was a good intro to how the computer industry works."

"You're welcome."

Her air of vulnerability both attracted and amused him. He wondered whether her regular dates ended with awkward moments like this.

Abruptly, he pulled his mind back from the irritating thought of her out with other men. To hell with other guys and what they'd done or hadn't. *He* wanted to kiss her.

He leaned in, but she dodged with a nervous laugh. He looked at her quizzically.

"You haven't been keeping to your part of the bargain," she said.

"Huh?" He blinked.

"Even though I learned a lot tonight about the computer-software industry in general, I didn't get a smidgen of information about Whittaker Enterprises in particular." Her chin came up. "What's your interest in Tim and Ben's company?"

And what an attractive chin it was, he thought. Attached to a long and graceful neck that led down to breasts straight out of an erotic fantasy. *His* erotic fantasy.

"Are you paying attention?"

"Mmm-hmm. Yeah." He focused his gaze on her face again. "I agreed to give you broad access, but *not* to give away confidential information about Whittaker's possible future plans. For one thing, you're the press. For another, that information could be very valuable on the stock market."

"Are you suggesting I'd do something illegal like purchasing company stock on an inside tip?" she asked crossly.

He tapped her nose. "Not you personally, no, but the policy still stands. The last thing I need is for inside information to inadvertently leak, so the fewer people who know anything, the better." She was too cute standing there, looking all mad at him. "But here's a hint I'm willing to give—nanotechnology."

"That's it?" she said disbelievingly. "One word?"

He couldn't help smiling as he leaned down again. "Yeah," he murmured. "But don't worry. There's more where that came from."

The kiss he gave her was brief, yet still powerful and disturbing, and he wondered again what he was doing getting mixed up with a journalist who just saw him as a convenient ticket to a promotion.

"I can't believe it!" her sister said. "Two guys who have great odds of seeing their bank accounts shoot into the multimillions and you didn't even mention you had a single and unattached younger sister? Did it even cross your mind that I have student loans to pay off? No, of course not," Samantha answered herself, before slumping into a chair. "You were too focused on Mr. Naughty-and-Nice."

"I was not focused on Noah," Kayla said absently.

Samantha snorted. "Yeah, right. I suppose that's why you've mentioned him about fifty times in the past hour?"

Kayla closed out of the website that she was viewing and looked away from the screen. It was a sunny Sunday afternoon and, as happened from time to time, Samantha had crashed at her place the night before, not wanting to take a late train back to school after an evening out on the town. "You're a real smarty-pants, you know?"

"Smart and *poor*," Samantha replied, then nodded at the computer. "What have you been doing?"

"Looking up everything I can find on the Internet about nanotechnology. As I said, it's the only hint he gave me."

If Noah had held better to his part of the bargain on Friday night, she wouldn't have to be looking up stuff. She couldn't believe he'd left her with a one-word hint!

They had just over three more weeks ahead of them, and he'd pony up or there'd be consequences. And, there wouldn't be any more kissing. If he hadn't caught her off guard, the kiss on Friday night would never have happened. She was a reporter doing a story, and he was her subject, for Pete's sake.

Still, truth be told, wasn't she partly to blame? She'd let herself get swept up in the mood of the evening.

She'd become attuned to every brush of his leg against hers, every smile that lit up his face, every nuance of conversation. So much so that she'd lost track of her mission, which was to get information on Whittaker Enterprises.

Of course, then there'd been that near brush with a photographer to distract her. She'd been hoping she could shadow him for a story without attracting the attention of the press. She definitely hadn't anticipated drawing media attention on their first outing together.

And then, to top it off, he'd kissed her—and she'd enjoyed it. *She'd wanted more.*

Good grief. She had to get a grip. She reminded herself that Noah Whittaker was a smooth-talking and accomplished seducer.

"So what's wrong with Noah?" Samantha asked.

"Nothing!" Then, because she realized she'd practically shouted, she took a deep breath. "Nothing."

"He's only wealthy, good-looking, smart—"

"Stop! He's also irritating, smug, arrogant, born with a silver spoon in his mouth and way too used to having women fall at his feet. I'm only trying to get a story here, okay? I am *not* interested in Noah."

"If you say so. You know, denial of physical chemistry is often the first step in a romantic relationship."

"Argh!" Kayla exclaimed in exasperation. Ever since Samantha had started majoring in psychology—supplemented by a steady diet of popular self-help books with titles such as *From Toxic Dates to Toxic Hate*—it had been "get in touch with your emotions" *this* and "express your feelings" *that*.

Her sister regarded her thoughtfully from her position in an overstuffed armchair. "You know, not every rich guy is a cad. Just because Mom made a mistake—"

"It wasn't a simple mistake. It was a catastrophe that sent her life reeling off course."

"Yes, but she got you in the process, and I don't think she's ever regretted that."

Kayla tamped down the wellspring of feeling that her sister's comment aroused. True, she'd always had a great relationship with her mother, but she couldn't forget the hard years they'd endured, years during which her mother had completed her college degree at night *and* raised a child as a single parent. Even with the help of her family, it had been hard.

"Have you heard anything about him recently?" Samantha asked.

"Who?" she responded, though she knew perfectly well what her sister meant. "Bentley Mathison IV?" She hadn't thought about her biological father in a while.

Her sister nodded.

"No." She busied herself straightening the papers on her computer desk. "He and his wife retreated to a luxury cottage on Martha's Vineyard after he was released from prison. He's been keeping a low profile ever since."

Which was fortunate for her. The chances she'd run into him at some gala or other that she had to cover for the *Sentinel* were slim—though, of course, he wouldn't recognize her since he'd never been involved in her life and she now used the common surname Jones.

When the apartment's buzzer sounded, Samantha said, "I'll get it," and popped out of her chair.

"Who is it?" she said into the intercom mounted on the entryway wall.

"Noah Whittaker," came the reply, unmistakable even though garbled by static.

Samantha turned, eyes wide with excitement. "It's—"

"I heard," Kayla said dryly. Her stomach did a somersault. Why was he here?

Samantha spoke into the intercom again. "Come on up." She pressed a button to let Noah in.

Kayla looked down at her sweatshirt and tights. She

was a mess and Mr. Lady-killer was coming up in the elevator.

"Quick!" Samantha said, jumping into action and pulling Kayla out of her chair. "Into the bedroom," she said, shoving her along. "Jeans tight, blouse low-cut, and put on some lipstick! Think *Cosmo* ad—casual but ready to frolic."

Thrust into her bedroom, Kayla turned around and started to protest.

"I'll stall him as long as I can," Samantha said and shut the door in her face.

Five

Noah knocked and, a full minute later, the door to the apartment opened and a knockoff of Kayla stood in front of him. She was wearing a T-shirt that had Tufts Field Hockey in big letters on the front, and her hair was caught up in a ponytail.

"Wow, look who has a license to thrill," she said, leaning against the door jamb. She stuck out her hand. "Hi, I'm Samantha, Kayla's sister."

Noah broke into a grin as he grasped the proffered hand. "I'm—"

"Mr. Naughty-and-Nice," she finished for him. "I know."

"What?" he spluttered on a laugh.

"Never mind," she said, pulling him in. "Can I get you something to drink? Beer? Wine? Sangria?"

"A beer is fine. Thanks."

"Kayla's in the bedroom changing into something comfortable," Samantha said as she walked into the small kitchen next to the entry. "She's been working all morning."

Noah noticed she didn't say Kayla had been *at* work all morning, but he limited himself to saying, "She's too intense."

"Well, she's going through her blond-ambition stage," Samantha said, opening the fridge.

Noah leaned a shoulder against the archway to the kitchen. "Don't you mean blind ambition?"

"That too." Samantha took a beer out of the fridge. "She's a real blonde by the way, in case anyone's interested." She opened a drawer and pulled out a bottle opener. "Ask me anything. I'll tell you everything you want to know. Well, almost everything."

"Samantha!" Kayla exclaimed aghast.

Noah glanced through the pass-through between the kitchen and the dining/living room. Kayla had emerged dressed in blue jeans and a short-sleeved, deep-red top. The scoop neck, he noticed, did amazing things for her cleavage.

"What?" Samantha asked, directing her question at her sister.

Noah felt his lips curve at Kayla's answering frown. "I like your sister," he said. "She's a firecracker."

"Really?" Samantha said.

At the same time, Kayla muttered, "That's not all she is."

Samantha leaned against the kitchen counter. "I hear you know a lot of up-and-coming types in the computer industry." Without missing a beat, she added, "I'm five-seven and a college junior, and I *love* meeting new people."

The hint was as subtle as a sledgehammer. "Yeah, I meet with some Silicon Valley types," he responded, enjoying himself, not the least because Kayla continued to look discomfited, "but most of them are, uh, wardrobe challenged." And that was the tip of the iceberg.

"I'm great with clothes," Samantha countered. "In fact, I sometimes advise Kayla."

"Do I have you to thank for the baby-doll top?"

"That's right. You owe me one." She handed him an open beer.

"All right, that's enough," Kayla said.

"Is she always like this?" Noah asked Samantha.

"Not always, no."

"She's too serious," Noah said, and they both looked at Kayla.

"And you're never serious," Kayla retorted.

"I'm studiedly unserious. It takes a lot of work," he replied lazily, pushing away from his spot in the entryway to the kitchen and moving into the living room.

"Right. Well, I prefer the terms *sensible* and *level-headed*." With a pointed look at him and her sister, she added, "Some of us need to be."

The first thing that caught his eye in her living room was the bouquet of roses on an end table. *His* roses.

She followed his gaze and stiffened. "They were too beautiful to throw out, but I didn't want them sitting around the office drawing attention." She shrugged. "Why look a gift horse in the mouth?"

He pulled his gaze away from the flowers. For some reason, he felt ridiculously pleased she hadn't chucked them in the trash bin. And the fact that he felt that way was, well, ridiculous.

"Here," he said, holding out a shawl. "You left this on the back seat of my car on Friday night."

"Thanks." She took the flimsy, sparkly material from him.

He shrugged. "I was driving through your neighborhood and figured I'd drop it off." He also hadn't been able to stop thinking about her. "I'd have called first, but I couldn't locate a number for you other than work."

From the corner of his eye, he noticed Samantha was following the conversation while pouring herself a glass of orange juice.

"Also, it gives me an opportunity to mention an event I have coming up."

"Oh?"

"Juice, Kayla?"

"Thanks, just water." To him, she said, "Have a seat."

He took the couch while she sat in an armchair.

He glanced around the apartment. It was small but thoughtfully furnished. On the walls hung framed black-and-white photo reprints of cityscapes: New York, Paris,

Boston, Miami, Sydney. Near the pass-through to the kitchen sat a black lacquer-and-glass table. The rest of the room consisted of an armchair, a cream-colored couch, a small television and a computer desk. The computer was a late-model Apple with a flat screen, salsa music emanating at a low volume from its two small speakers.

He nodded at the computer. "You've got some eclectic musical tastes. From Norah Jones to salsa?"

"We were raised on salsa," Samantha piped up as she walked over to Kayla with a glass of water. "Our grandmother is a big fan." Samantha looked at him. "She was born in Cuba."

"Was she?" Noah took a sip of his beer, amused that the expression on Kayla's face said she wondered whether her sister was planning to give him details about their *entire* family.

"Yup," Samantha said, ignoring her sister's pointed look and sitting down on the couch next to her. "Bolero, salsa, merengue—*Abuela* likes it all. Kayla and I could barely get anything else played around the house since our grandmother was often there. Fortunately, Ricky Martin hit it big, and we finally found a middle ground."

"Interesting," he murmured, looking at Kayla.

"*Abuela* sang around the house, too," Samantha continued, then laughed before turning to her sister, "but Kayla only sings in the shower."

"Yeah, I know."

"So, you mentioned an event a minute ago," Kayla said, clearly looking to change the subject. "What event?"

"There's a black-tie benefit for the Boston Esplanade being thrown on the banks of the Charles River next Saturday night by the Charlesbank Association. I'd like you to come with me. You'll get to listen in on some interesting conversations."

"Unless it's a costume ball with Venetian masks, the answer is no. We had one near brush with paparazzi on Friday night. I'll follow you around but in a more low-key way from now on."

He sat back and tilted his head. "Somehow I thought that would be your initial reaction."

"Good, then you weren't disappointed," she countered.

Samantha was looking like she longed for a big tub of popcorn so she could watch the gathering storm with the same intensity she'd view an absorbing TV drama.

"Instead of inviting me to charity benefits," Kayla continued, "if you really wanted to help me, you'd be inviting me to tour Whittaker Enterprises' offices and giving me a list of employees to speak with."

"Fine. I've been too busy this week to get to that," he responded. "Call my office on Monday. We'll set up a time for you to come by and I'll have some names for you. But I still want you to go to the Charlesbank Association event with me."

"Going to a charity benefit with you would be like waving a red flag in front of the gossip columnists in this town—they're sure to charge, and odds are we'd be gored."

"I'll introduce you as the reporter who's researching an in-depth piece on Whittaker Enterprises," he said with patience. "Everyone will buy it because the alternative—that we're flaunting a relationship that I just publicly denied existed—will seem too outrageous."

Kayla rolled her eyes. "Wow, you sure know nothing about gossip columnists. Stories about three-headed aliens landing on top of city hall aren't too outrageous." She leaned forward. "And if the mayor refutes it, of course, the headline is Mayor Denies Aliens Landed on his Roof."

Samantha laughed.

Noah stared at Kayla, and she stared right back.

Sighing, he turned to Samantha. "Feel free to chime in any time, kid. I could use all the help I can get."

"No way." Samantha shook her head. "Kayla's wearing her 'look.' She can be very stubborn when she wants to be."

"You don't say?" he said, not taking his eyes off Kayla.

"Yup. She's been known to camp out overnight for concert tickets."

"Everyone has his price," he said.

"You couldn't afford me," Kayla retorted.

"How do you know what I can afford?" he responded coolly. "Done a lot of research on me?"

She looked away.

He wasn't sure why he was pressing her to accept his invitation, except somewhere along the way getting close to Kayla had taken on an importance equal to rehabilitating his image. "You need to be there. It'll be full of glitterati and beautiful people."

"I can get a press pass."

"I'll introduce you to people who are worth knowing. I'll even put in a good word. Some of them have a natural aversion to goss—uh, journalists."

"Who?" she asked doubtfully.

Ah, finally, Noah thought, a chink in the armor: getting the upper hand in her ongoing rivalry with Sybil LaBreck was enticing. "Susan Bennington-Walsh," he said, naming one of Boston's leading hostesses.

She shook her head. "Already know her."

"You don't say." Surprising. "Susan disdains the press, and gossip columnists in particular."

"That's what they all say, at least publicly," she replied dryly.

"Are you saying she secretly feeds information to you?"

"No comment."

Well, well. He filed away that bit of information and reminded himself not to say anything too revealing at one of Susan's future parties. "The mayor then," he offered, switching tactics.

"You know the mayor?" Samantha said, looking impressed.

"Of course he knows the mayor," Kayla responded.

"I contributed to his last election campaign."

"Handsomely, I'm sure," Kayla jibed.

"Naturally." He could tell Kayla was mulling over how a personal introduction to the mayor would benefit a would-be business reporter.

Finally, she said doubtfully, "Black tie or business attire?"

He masked a grin. "Black tie."

"Great!" Samantha clapped her hands together, not giving her sister a chance to shy away again. "Now that that's settled, tell me about your racing career, Noah. I'd love to know what it's like to race at two-hundred miles an hour."

Noah gave her a quick grin. No doubt about it, he thought, the kid had charm in spades. Too bad he had a major case of the hots for her sister, who seemed determined to keep him at arm's length.

"I'm sure Noah has better things to do," Kayla interjected.

"Trying to get rid of me?" he asked.

Their eyes met and clashed.

"Don't be silly," she retorted. "I'm only thinking of you and your busy schedule."

"Come on, Noah," Samantha pleaded, ignoring her sister. "It all sounds so thrilling."

"Thrilling and dangerous," he corrected. Certainly no one knew that better than he did. Danger—of the fatal variety—was what had convinced him that it was time to put away his racing suit.

Samantha curled up on the couch. "How did you get started?"

He shrugged, having fielded similar questions countless times before from fans, acquaintances and the merely curious. "At a racing school, like a lot of other professional drivers. I got the appropriate racing licenses and started driving in some of the lower-level series and then worked my way up to an Indy car."

"Did you race in the Indianapolis 500?"

"Yeah, I had a couple of starts there." More than that, he'd had a top-five finish in his rookie season. He'd been red hot until the crash that had changed his life and put an end to his professional racing career at the relatively young age of twenty-six.

Samantha continued to look impressed. "How do you get into the big leagues?"

"It's tough," he admitted. "You need high speeds even to qualify for the big events. Then you throw in finding a racing team that will give you a car, lining up sponsors, putting together a pit crew, and everything else."

"So why bother?" Kayla asked.

He glanced over at her. "The thrill."

There wasn't anything like taking a turn at two-hundred miles an hour, fighting to stay in control of the car, and making split-second decisions that meant the difference between winning and losing.

He didn't expect her to understand. His family hadn't, though they'd come to accept his dream of racing cars.

The love of speed, he'd found, was something you were either born with or weren't. In his case, there must have been a genetic mutation because no one else in his upper-crust Boston Brahmin family thought that hurtling yourself through space at two-hundred-plus miles an hour was a pleasant way to spend a sunny afternoon.

He caught Kayla observing him with a thoughtful expression on her face.

"For me, a thrill means finding a Stella McCartney designer top in my size at a thrift shop," Samantha said.

Noah laughed. "Can't say I can relate, but I'm often appreciative of the results."

Samantha grinned back; Kayla scowled.

Holding Samantha's gaze, he nodded his head at Kayla. "She doesn't like my playboy ways."

"Maybe I just don't like you," Kayla retorted.

"Ouch." He pretended to wince.

Samantha leaned forward confidingly. "It's not personal. She just doesn't like any rich—"

"Okay!" Kayla said, then stood up and shot her sister a dire look.

Samantha clamped her mouth shut.

Baffled, he looked from Kayla to Samantha. "She just doesn't like any—?"

"Rich men who ask probing questions," Kayla finished flatly.

He looked up at Kayla and knew, just knew, he needed to know more. He needed to know everything about her, to know her intimately. And he wasn't giving up.

On the following Wednesday morning, Kayla showed up early at Whittaker Enterprises' headquarters. She'd arranged with Noah to tour the company's offices, talk to people, follow him around and, basically, see how things operated.

She'd taken extra-special care with her clothes and makeup. She'd already discovered the hard way that, for a good chunk of the world, *young single female* meant *not to be taken seriously*.

So, today she'd paired navy flare-leg trousers with a striped blue-and-yellow open-collar shirt. Her jewelry was discreet and understated, just a watch and some small cubic-zirconia stud earrings.

The look was classy but professional, or at least she hoped so. As Ms. Rumor-Has-It, she had to dress the part, but this was something different altogether.

On the drive over to Noah's office, she'd reflected again on the research she'd done and the articles she'd read on Whittaker Enterprises—and on Noah himself— in preparation for today's visit.

Whittaker Enterprises had been started by Noah's father back in the 1960s and had since metamorphosed into a conglomerate with interests primarily in real estate and high technology. Noah's oldest brother, Quentin, had taken over the reins of the family company a few years back, when his father had moved into semi-retirement. At the same time, Noah had become the point person for Whittaker Enterprises' computer business. That was, as soon as he'd quelled his maverick tendencies. After graduating from M.I.T. with a bachelor's degree in computer science, instead of joining the family business, he'd headed off to pursue a race-car driving career.

She'd found news articles from the time that detailed the surprise with which Noah's move had been greeted in Boston social circles. It was as if he'd announced he'd rather be the jockey than the horse owner. *It just wasn't done.* Not in the rarified circles of Boston old-line families.

Still, he'd entered the Indy car-racing circuit. After three years of heady success had come the accident that had marked the end of his career. Precisely, it had happened on turn three at the Michigan Indy 400. Noah had been fighting for the lead with Jack Gillens, one of his racing buddies. Just as Noah was going by him, Jack had lost control of his car and hit the barrier wall on the racing oval head-on; car debris had gone flying everywhere.

Attempts at resuscitating Jack had proved futile. Minutes after the crash, the race had finished under a yellow flag. Noah had won, only to learn Jack had been taken to the hospital but had been declared dead upon arrival. A later investigation had concluded Noah wasn't to blame for the crash.

Until the accident seven years ago, Noah had been in the news a lot. He had sex appeal in spades, and that, combined with his high-testosterone racing career, had been enough to net him a dozen magazine covers and have him named one of *People*'s Sexiest Men Alive.

But after the accident, he'd holed up. Then, after a few months, he'd made a public announcement that he was retiring from racing. He'd gone back to M.I.T., gotten his doctorate in computer science and then joined the family firm.

He dropped out of the public eye for a short time after the accident, but he came back with a vengeance. In his new incarnation as a playboy, he was seen squiring around models, actresses and, yes, even a reality-show contestant. He was back making regular appearances in *People* magazine, in *Us Weekly* and in the local gossip columns.

Kayla had known about the accident, of course. People talked, still.

But she hadn't known the details of the fatal crash or of Noah's life at the time. She'd still been in college at that point. However, having read the news articles, the past—Noah's past—was all very fresh for her.

She remembered his reaction back at the book-launch party when she'd brought up the racing accident—he'd shut down immediately—and she cringed inwardly again.

And, as she walked around Whittaker Enterprises with Noah, everything she'd read was at the back of her mind.

"I've been doing some research on nanotechnology," she said conversationally.

"Really?" he said. "What have you discovered?"

"Probably lots of things I should have been hearing from you instead."

He laughed.

"So," she said, "instead of my telling you what *I've discovered,* why don't you tell me what *you know*?"

"All right. Have you heard of Moore's Law?"

"No."

"Okay, well, Moore's Law basically says data density in computers will double about every eighteen months or so."

She nodded. "How does Moore's Law relate to nanotechnology?"

"I'm getting there," he said, giving her an amused look. "If you've done your homework, you know nanotechnology concerns the manipulation of atoms. It gets its name from the fact that the structures it studies—atoms and the like—are measured in nanometers. A nanometer is one-billionth of a meter."

"Right." So far everything he'd said was in line with her research.

"The potential applications for nanotechnology are practically limitless, from handheld supercomputers to faster diagnoses for cancer."

"Wow."

"Exactly. People in the computing field are racing each other to harness and use nanotechnology, even though it's still a young field. It wasn't until the mid-1980s that a scanning tunneling microscope was developed that could study atoms. But now nanotechnology is the biggest thing since computers."

"Are you saying that Whittaker Enterprises has developed a product that uses nanotechnology?"

He smiled. "I haven't gotten to that part of the story yet. You'll have to stay tuned."

"But—"

"Come on," he said, interrupting her, "let me introduce you to people and then get out of your way. You'll start to get a picture of what we're all about."

She sighed. At least she'd made some progress. "Okay, great."

Noah, she soon learned, had organized the computer side of the business into project teams, each headed by a team leader. The teams were small groups flexible enough to make things happen.

She jotted notes as she talked to people. One group

had developed a new, ultra-slim handheld PDA that was about to launch on the market. Another was testing a super-light portable DVD player. *Small* seemed to be the name of the game. However, no one brought up nano-technology in any detail. She got the sense *that* information was rather sensitive.

Everyone, however, sang Noah's praises. He was smart, easy to work with, unflappable and had enough stamina to work around the clock if necessary—all of which, of course, she felt compelled to bring up later when she caught up with Noah outside his office.

"So, apparently your reputation is that you work hard and party harder."

He smiled. "You sound annoyed."

"It's the kiss of death for reporters. No dish, no dirt, no anything."

He held up his hands. "Hey, I didn't tell them to hold back, just to keep their mouths shut about confidential business information."

"Everyone's afraid of antagonizing the boss, I bet."

He shook his head. "Our attrition rates are very low for the industry, and we pay top dollar. People are here because they want to be here." When she had no ready reply he said, "Come on, I'll take you to lunch."

She reluctantly accepted. Lunch, as it turned out, was not in the building's well-stocked cafeteria, which she'd passed earlier in the day, but in Carlyle, at a charming little bistro.

She ordered the French onion soup, a half sandwich and a healthy serving of information from Noah.

He just laughed and ordered the crab cakes.

"So," she said after their food had arrived and they'd dug in, "I've been reading a lot about you."

He raised his eyebrows. "You're not writing about me anymore in your column, so what's there to read these days?"

"I meant about your past. I've been coming across articles while researching Whittaker Enterprises."

His eyes flickered. "The past can't be changed, so I don't spend too much time examining it myself."

"You had a great racing career going," she said. "I didn't realize how successful you were until I went back through the news reports."

He wiped his mouth with his napkin and took his time answering. "What? Would it have changed how you wrote about me in your column?"

"I don't know," she admitted. She hadn't realized Noah had been such close buddies with the driver who'd been killed. It made sense though: they'd belonged to the same racing team. "It would have given me a different perspective though."

He seemed to wait for her to go on.

"Auto racing seemed like an odd choice for you."

He shrugged. "You're not the first person to make that observation. The truth is, though, there are a lot of similarities between auto racing and what I do now. Professional auto racing is all about the technology."

"How did you even get interested in it?"

"In a word?"

"Yes."

"Go-carts."

She raised her eyebrows. For once, he was looking earnest, instead of using his customary half-amused expression.

"It was a friend's birthday party," he explained. "It took place at a racetrack, and we got to race around in these little carts. I was hooked."

"And you were how old?"

"Ten. I moved up to real cars in my teens. Took a hiatus from competitive racing for a while in college, and then I was back at it."

"Until the accident," she corrected.

He sat back, took a breath and then expelled it slowly. "Yeah?"

He said it like a challenge.

"Why did you choose to quit? From the articles I read, you were a hot commodity, poised for a great career if not the record books."

"Maybe it wasn't a choice. Some things aren't. If the highest card you're dealt is a ten, you can't put a king in play."

She looked at him. Was he kidding her? He was gorgeous, wealthy and talented. "Most people would look at you and say you definitely got dealt a king in the card game of life."

"Most people don't know me," he said, then added pointedly, "even if they think they do based on what they read or write about me."

She took the jab and kept going. "They don't need to know you to understand you grew up privileged—"

"Yeah, but sometimes it doesn't matter how wealthy you are, you still have to deal with the irrevocable moments of life."

"Is that what the accident was? Something you wish you could take back if you could? Is that why you threw away the racing career?"

He motioned the waiter for their check, then looked back and studied her for a second. "Maybe it was the other way around. Maybe the racing career threw me away. Or, maybe, *Kayla*—" he said, drawing out her name "—I just decided I didn't want to race for the next ten or twenty years and that developing cutting-edge technology was more appealing."

He was the closest to really ticked off that she'd ever seen him, and that included the time of their confrontation at the book-launch party. She shifted in her seat.

He narrowed his eyes. "I hope there isn't some sort of strange reporter's instinct at play here. You know, digging for some weird psychological profile for your article."

She hadn't been thinking about that—had only wanted to have her curiosity slaked—but now that he mentioned it…. "And what if there is? Is the accident the reason you became the hard-partying Noah of the past few years?"

After signing the check, he looked up. "You're barking up the wrong tree. If you really want to understand what makes the techie guy in me tick, then look at my experiences at M.I.T. and at the office, not on the racetrack."

She wasn't so sure about that. Not so sure at all.

Six

There was no place to hide.

She'd looked.

A party hosted under a white tent afforded no inviting nooks and crannies into which a single woman seeking to avoid a fate worse than death could cram herself. Particularly a woman dressed in a sequined halter top and black sheath skirt and two-and-a-half-inch heels. For the sake of future events, she'd have to make a polite suggestion to the Charlesbank Association.

The evening had started off innocuously enough. Noah had picked her up, appearing more sinfully good-looking in a tux than any man had a right to look. Her pulse had kicked up a notch, a response that she was growing used to. She'd come to admit to herself that, yes, okay, she did find him very attractive—who wouldn't? But she knew better than to think that acting on any attraction between them was a good idea, recent kisses aside.

Once they'd arrived at the charity benefit, Noah, as promised, had introduced her to the mayor as a journalist who worked for the *Boston Sentinel* and who was gathering material for an in-depth profile on Whittaker Enterprises. Fortunately, the mayor had not seemed to connect her face to the Ms. Rumor-Has-It column. And Noah had been right: with his introduction and implicit endorsement, the mayor had been friendly and approachable.

Unfortunately, though, after that brief interlude, the evening had turned from one where she was playing with nice, friendly dolphins to one where she was swimming with the sharks.

First, she'd run into Fluffy, who'd been eager to make sure Kayla would mention her in Monday's column.

Then Buffy the Man Slayer had homed in on Noah. Evidently, she'd taken to heart the hint in Kayla's column and decided Noah would make a lovely addition to her all-male menagerie.

Kayla was thankful Huffy, at least, wasn't around to add to the drama. According to word of mouth, she was still in Europe, presently flirting with a German count who was dancing attendance on her. Kayla had no doubt the two of them would soon hit the European gossip magazines.

Kayla wondered whether Noah would be crushed by

the news. She glanced over at him now and caught his look of mild irritation from across the room, where Sybil LaBreck had run him to ground.

Under other circumstances, Kayla might have felt some pity. Under present ones, however, she was too busy dealing with her own problems.

Because, just as she'd been breathing a sigh of relief, she'd turned around and spotted Bentley Mathison IV.

For an instant, she'd frozen. Then she'd embarked on her present and so-far-fruitless search for a hiding spot.

Bentley Mathison and his wife wouldn't recognize her, but she still had no interest in encountering them. Particularly here. Particularly now.

Giving up on the tent, she headed toward an exit. She could take a moment outside to collect herself.

As she made her way toward a gap in the tent, she recognized Noah's siblings as they entered along with their spouses, and groaned at the timing.

Trapped, she made a complete 360-degree turn, looking for at least a potted plant that might afford some camouflage.

Noah, she noticed, had disentangled himself from Sybil's clutches and was heading her way. His family, with Allison Whittaker in the lead, was bearing down on her from the opposite direction. And, she noticed, Bentley Mathison and his wife were making their way toward all of them, too.

She dredged up a smile. It was the least she could do when her life was bearing down on her with all the horror of an impending train wreck.

"Noah!"

"Allison!"

"Kayla!"

Help! Kayla thought.

"Well, isn't this a pleasant surprise," Allison said. "We didn't know you'd be here, Noah." Allison looked for affirmation at the dangerously good-looking man next to her.

Kayla knew Connor Rafferty by sight. Rumor had it that he'd carried a torch for Allison for years before they'd recently begun seeing each other and gotten married.

Bringing up the rear, behind Connor, was a tall, dark-haired man who looked as if he'd stepped off the pages of *GQ* magazine and whom Kayla knew by sight to be Noah's older brother Matt.

Behind Matt, Kayla noticed that Noah's other brother, Quentin, and his wife, Liz—whom she knew from various social functions that she'd covered in the past for the *Sentinel*—had already been waylaid by a couple of other guests nearer the tent's entrance.

Noah shrugged. "Until recently, I wasn't sure I'd be showing up either."

Allison looked from Noah to Kayla, zeroing in on the arm that Noah had just slipped around her waist and was using to guide her forward.

She couldn't blame Allison for looking confused. After all, mere days ago, Kayla had been the bane of Noah's existence.

"Allison, Connor, Matt, this is Kayla."

Allison reacted first. "Kayla and I have been introduced to each other before." She looked at her brother, her lips twitching upward. "I'm just surprised Kayla's here with you."

Kayla felt herself grow warm, but Noah said, "I guess you haven't heard that Kayla is shadowing me because she's doing a profile on Whittaker Enterprises for the *Boston Sentinel*."

Allison raised her eyebrows, and Connor and Matt, though they refrained from making any comment, wore looks that said they found it all highly entertaining.

Allison opened her mouth to speak, but, before she could say anything, a voice caused all of them to turn.

Bentley Mathison, who until now had remained quiet, spoke up. "Noah and Matthew Whittaker." He stepped forward, hand outstretched and chuckling too heartily to sound sincere. "How long has it been?"

Kayla winced. Bentley Mathison's audacity was stupendous, especially in light of the fact that, if it had been a long time, it was entirely due to his thirty-six months spent behind bars for tax evasion and misappropriation of funds.

"Bentley," Noah said, nodding in acknowledgment and, reluctantly, it seemed to Kayla, accepting the proffered hand. "Yes, it's been a while."

"Too long," Bentley said jovially. He then turned to greet the other Whittaker siblings and introduce them to his wife, Margaux.

Allison, Kayla noticed, appeared cool during the introductions. And, no wonder, Kayla thought. As an assistant district attorney who'd recently been harassed by a defendant in one of her cases—before Connor had reportedly led the police to the culprit—she doubtlessly did not suffer criminals, past or present, gladly.

When Noah turned and introduced Kayla to the Mathisons, she tried to appear unaffected. Nevertheless, her hand was clammy and cold as it was grasped by Bentley Mathison's.

Her biological father.

She looked into his pale blue eyes—as clear and cold as a winter sky—and could not believe this was the man who'd set her life on its trajectory, and, in fact, the man responsible for her very existence.

Unbidden and uninvited, her mind busied itself looking for resemblances. She dreaded finding any.

She caught Noah looking at her oddly.

It was then she realized she'd been holding on to Bentley Mathison's hand.

Embarrassed, she murmured, "Nice to meet you," and then withdrew her hand.

She was vaguely aware of conversation continuing to flow around her, but she was in a weird state where she heard everything but took in nothing. Mostly she faintly discerned that Bentley was attempting to ingratiate himself with the Whittakers—probably in the hopes of resuscitating business contacts—and that the Whittakers were responding with varying degrees of polite detachment.

No one apparently noticed how uncomfortable she'd become. No one except Noah, apparently, since she caught him tossing her a quizzical look or two.

At some point, she heard Noah say, "Excuse us." Then, without waiting for a response, he tugged her toward the dance floor. He guided her into his arms and they started swaying to a slow tune.

"What was that all about?" he asked finally against her hair.

"What?" She tilted her head back to look up at him.

"Your Medusa impersonation when you were introduced to Bentley Mathison. I thought you were going to turn him to stone."

"Don't be ridiculous. If I did have a reaction, it's only because the man is a shameless unreformed criminal."

He raised his eyebrows. "Strong words."

"Your sister seemed to have a similar reaction."

"Yeah, but she's in the business of being the scourge of society's criminal element. You, on the other hand, are in the business of getting information however you can get it."

"Not from Bentley Mathison," she said sharply. Then added less stridently, "And since when are you befriending former criminals?"

"Hey, hey," he said soothingly. "I didn't say I like the guy. I just wasn't going to create a scene when he approached me in the middle of a charity gala. Besides, he paid his debt to society by serving his prison sentence."

She looked away. "Maybe there are other debts that are still outstanding."

"What?" Noah asked.

Realizing she'd muttered aloud, she said, "Never

mind. I don't want to talk about it." The last thing she wanted to do was give Noah Whittaker more personal information about herself.

He looked like he wanted to argue with her, but then he simply nodded.

They danced in silence. And, despite being distracted by the presence of Bentley Mathison, she felt an electric awareness course through her at Noah's nearness. Being pressed against his muscular frame, she experienced a strange fluttery sensation in her midsection.

When the song ended, he guided her off the dance floor. "Now, let's get back to you and Bentley Mathison."

It took her a second to digest what he'd said, caught up as she still was in the sensation of having been held against him. She gave him a sidelong look. "There's nothing to tell. It's just too bad even a prison sentence doesn't mean social disgrace anymore."

He shrugged. "Maybe disgrace is in the eye of the beholder."

"Too true," she said, half to herself.

Just then she noticed Bentley Mathison was standing in their path along with his wife and another couple. If they continued walking on as they were, they'd be forced back into conversation with him, and from the looks of it, that's what Mathison was hoping for.

She stopped and clutched Noah's arm.

He looked down at her, a question in his eyes. "What?" He cut himself off as he looked up again and caught sight of Bentley Mathison.

Glancing back at her, he muttered, "All right, you want to come clean about this?"

She gave a small defeated nod. "But first get me out of here." Her voice sounded strained to her own ears.

In a deft maneuver, he turned, pretended to recognize someone across the room, and half pulled, half dragged her along with him as he strode past several tables.

They were outside the tent within minutes, and she took a deep breath.

"You okay?" Noah asked, and she was surprised to see genuine concern etched on his face. "You look pale."

"Fine…I'm fine." She took another breath, then said in a rush, "Bentley Mathison is my biological father but he doesn't know it."

Noah raised his eyebrows, then stuffed his hands in his pockets. "Your secrets pack a punch, I'll say that."

"Sometimes I wish I didn't have any."

"Then why keep any?" he said.

She looked at him askance. "It's not easy telling someone that my ancestry is one-quarter Cuban, one-quarter English, and one-half jerk."

"You're not the jerk. He is," he said with conviction.

She was close to tears and wondering now what had possessed her to blurt out one of her most closely-held secrets. And to Noah, of all people! Why, all he had to do was relay that juicy tidbit to Sybil LaBreck and Kayla would be cooked, roasted over the open fire of the public's flaming need for scandal.

As if reading her mind, Noah said, "Don't worry, I

won't tell anyone, and especially not Sybil LaBreck." He looked around. "Let's get out of here. I'll take you home."

"But we arrived only a short time ago."

He took her arm. "You're in no shape to go back in there and face Bentley and company, not to mention Buffy the Man Slayer. And, for the record, neither am I. Let's go."

"Thanks." She was relieved he was taking charge, and surprised at his understanding.

She stole a glance at him. He was frowning and looking formidable. Yet, strangely, right this second, she found she liked him better than she ever had.

Noah flipped the light switch as they entered her apartment.

What a night. First, he'd been cornered by Buffy, then Sybil LaBreck had stopped him to ask irritating and probing questions about the true nature of his relationship with Kayla. She suspected all was not as it appeared, or at least as he'd been insisting publicly. He'd finally gotten rid of her with a dismissive comment.

And, to top off the evening, of course, he'd never have guessed Kayla was Bentley Mathison's biological daughter.

No wonder she seemed to have issues with men. Particularly rich, to-the-mansion-born types, a class into which he fell.

What was it that her sister had started to say before being cut off? Something about Kayla's dislike for him not being personal. After tonight, he understood why:

Kayla's issue was with all guys who bore a superficial similarity to Bentley Mathison.

Yet, the joke was on him. Because he'd been checking his symptoms and there was no doubt about it: he had a major case of lust for Kayla.

He watched as Kayla set her sequined purse on the table. With her back still to him, she lifted the hair from her neck and shook her head. He lapped up the view of her smooth, bare back before the curtain of sleek hair fell back into place.

He cleared his throat and she glanced back at him over her shoulder.

She looked doe-eyed and lost for a second. Her shoulders lowered. "Sorry, I'm being rude," she murmured.

"I was just going to ask if you needed anything. A glass of wine, coffee." Me.

He tamped down the well of lust that came unbidden with that last thought.

She forced a little laugh as she turned fully toward him. "Quite a role reversal. Those are things I should be asking you."

He just looked at her. She was good to look at, her shoulders toned in the top that she wore, her breasts round and full and her calves shapely beneath her long- ish skirt.

She broke the awkward silence by starting toward him. "I'll just get us both a drink. How's that?"

"Yeah, sure."

He should have moved back. Instead, he let her brush by him on the way to the kitchen.

The effect was electric. On him, anyway. Had he imagined the quiver that had gone through her?

He shoved his hands in his pockets to keep from grabbing and kissing her. Instead, he watched as she poured him a scotch on the rocks.

She set it on the kitchen counter near him. "There you go," she said without glancing at him.

Had she been afraid to touch him? He couldn't tell because she refused to look up.

He took the drink, then walked into the living room as he heard her open and close the refrigerator. He took a sip, felt the burn, then loosened his tie with one hand before raking his hair.

He felt more than heard her enter and turned to look at her. She came toward him, all cool Grace Kelly allure dressed up as 1950s bombshell, her stiletto heels clicking on the wood floor before hitting the area rug in front of the couch.

She held up her glass. "Cranberry juice with a splash of vodka." She clinked her glass to his. "Cheers."

A smile pulled at his lips. "Feeling reckless, are we?"

"Hmm." She shrugged. "Aren't you the expert on living dangerously?"

He took another sip, regarding her through narrowed eyes. "If I lived dangerously, I wouldn't be standing over here and you wouldn't be standing over there."

She smiled, a gleam in her eyes. "But I'm only inches away."

"Exactly." Tonight, it seemed, was the night for her to confront all the disreputable males in her life: her biological father, *him*. "Let's get to the bottom of what this is about, okay? Running into Bentley Mathison threw you for a loop."

"Mmm." She licked her lips.

He forced his mind to stay on topic.

She walked away. "So boring. Can we talk about something else?" She sat on the couch, crossed her legs and patted the seat next to her. "I don't understand how you got your reputation as a great seducer when you use lovely conversation starters like deadbeat, jailbird fathers."

He was tempted to show her just how he'd gotten his reputation, but her current performance could have rivaled Buffy the Man Slayer's. And, that's exactly what it was: a performance. She was playing the seductress— did she realize how naturally the role came to her?— intent on conquering him, the great seducer.

He swirled his drink. "Tell me how your mother fell under the spell of the great Bentley Mathison."

Kayla wrinkled her nose, then took a sip from her glass. The reckless gleam hadn't disappeared from her eyes. "It's a tragedy in three parts. I like comedies better, don't you?"

"How does act one begin?"

She heaved a sigh. "Act one begins with a young woman from a close-knit family going off to college on a scholarship."

"Your mother?"

"Mmm-hmm. She gets a summer job at a financial

services firm. Happily, it pays well and will help with the rest of her college bills. One of the partners takes a liking to her."

"Bentley."

"Yes, and reportedly quite the smooth operator even when he was younger."

"So," he guessed, "the summer intern proceeds to get pregnant by said partner, basking in the thrill of his attention."

"Yes, that would be act two." She swirled her drink. "You're too smart not to know act three."

"He refuses to have anything to do with her," he said flatly.

"Right," she confirmed, her tone harsh. "You see, Bentley was about to become engaged to the daughter of a well-connected financier. Of course, a connection like that was going to make his career."

"What happened to your mother?"

"Well, she was too afraid to tell anyone about the affair at first. Who would have believed her? Bentley had encouraged her to keep their relationship under wraps in order not to raise eyebrows at the office."

She shook her head, then went on. "But eventually she told her family. They took her in. She dropped out of school for a time to have the baby. With her family's help, though, she finally finished her degree."

"And your sister?"

"Well, there's the happy postscript." She put down her drink on the end table. "Several years on, the woman meets a man who's her soul mate. They fall in love and marry. He adopts her child and, later, they have a daughter together."

"Understood," he said, "except for one small detail."

"What's that?"

"I'm not Bentley," he said deliberately.

"I never said you were."

"No, but you act like it."

She uncrossed her legs and stood up, armor in place. "I get enough pop psychology from Samantha."

He wasn't letting her off the hook. "I got it wrong, didn't I?"

"Got what wrong?"

He shook his head and set his glass down, then let his gaze rake over her. "I'm not the favorite whipping boy of your column because you're secretly attracted to playboys. Just the opposite, in fact. Players remind you of your biological father, so you're determined to rake them over the coals."

She tossed her hair over her shoulder. "Believe what you want. You don't know me."

He sauntered closer. "Of course, that's too bad for me," he mused. "I prefer the story about your secret attraction to playboys."

She threw up her hands in exasperation and he caught her chin in his hand.

The air went out of her and her eyes widened. "What are you doing?" she said, stumbling over the words.

"Putting you to the test," he muttered, his gaze focused on her mouth.

"W-what test?"

"You know, the one where you prove that, unlike your mother, you can't be taken in and seduced by the cads of the world."

He raised his eyes to look into her stormy brown ones, and then he kissed her.

Seven

The second Noah's lips touched Kayla's, she felt herself yield. His kiss this time was not a fleeting brush, but a command. It took her breath away and her mouth opened under the pressure of his soft, coaxing lips.

He took the kiss deeper, his hands stroking up and down her arms, forcing her to deal with the emotions roiling inside her, forcing her to deal with *him*.

He was *so* wrong about her. She didn't write about him in her column because she had an ax to grind with player types who reminded her of Bentley Mathison.

If she wrote about Noah in her column, it was only because he led the type of glitzy private life that people liked to read about. Nothing more, except perhaps her own prejudice against someone whose glamorous and charmed life seemed so far from the everyday concerns of an average person like her.

She supposed he expected her to push him away now and break their kiss. Instead, she slid her arms around his neck.

She met him kiss for kiss.

She wasn't going to run away from his challenge. She'd seen the way he'd looked at her tonight. He'd eaten her up with his eyes. No, Noah was far from immune to her, and she knew she had good odds of being the seducer rather than the seduced.

His arm snaked around her and pulled her flush up against him. He was all hard planes and muscles, big and male. And aroused, she thought, as a shiver went through her.

He lifted his head and sucked in a breath. His gaze was hot and intent. "You're weakening," he said, his voice raspy and hoarse with sexual excitement.

"So are you." She sounded breathless.

"Just the invitation I needed," he murmured.

"It wasn't an invitation. It was a warning."

He laughed softly and nuzzled her temple, then trailed whisper-light kisses along the side of her face. "I'm a risk taker, remember?"

He blew lightly into her ear and she shuddered. She felt sensitized to his every move.

He kissed and then sucked on her earlobe before nibbling along her neck. One hand was splayed on her bare upper back; the other had gone to cup her backside, nestling her closer to his arousal.

Her head fell back to afford him better access and she closed her eyes. It was becoming harder to tell who was the seducer and who the seduced as they both became caught up in the moment.

Only when light fingers of cool air caressed her did she realize he'd lowered the zipper on her halter top, which now gaped around her to reveal her strapless black bra.

She sought his gaze.

His face was flushed, his gaze taking her in. "You're beautiful." He trailed his fingers along the satiny fabric of the bra. "Sexy. Like a Christmas package just waiting to be unwrapped."

Her breasts felt hot, heavy and tight under his hungry gaze, and a quivery warmth settled in her middle.

Then he was kissing her again, and she soon discovered that, not only was it unclear who was seducing whom, but it no longer seemed to matter.

All that did matter was that he continue to do wickedly pleasurable things to her. Because she wanted him with an intensity that surprised her.

When he'd finished unhooking her bra, he broke their kiss and sat on the edge of the couch behind him to kiss and nuzzle her breasts.

She ran her fingers through his hair, which felt soft, thick and inviting, and caressed his thigh, which felt hard and sinewy, the muscles bunched.

She moaned as he laved one nipple and then blew softly on it, sending all her nerve endings into overdrive in the process.

"Noah…"

"Shh," he said. "Don't think. Just feel."

He moved to her other breast, repeating his attention, as she shuddered against him.

It was too much and not enough.

Finally, he lifted his head. "You've got the most beautiful breasts I've ever seen," he said thickly. He traced the edge of one nipple, then the curve of her breast until she wanted to moan in response. "They're full but firm and uptilted. The nipples are tight and hot. Gorgeous."

His words sent heat coursing through her veins, arousing her even more. She tugged at his tuxedo tie until it hung loose and undone. "Let me see you."

Her hands went to the buttons of his shirt, while he shrugged out of his tux jacket. Once he'd gotten rid of his jacket and shirt, he pulled his white undershirt over his head and she was greeted by the sight of his smooth chest with its flat abs and defined muscles.

"Tit for tat. We're even," he said, his voice husky.

She ran her hands over his biceps, then trailed them over his chest. "You're in fantastic shape."

"I try even with my work schedule," he murmured back, cupping her face and drawing her down to him.

He kissed her deeply, giving her his tongue again and again, his hands on her breasts, then caressing her back, and then hiking her skirt so she could straddle his bent leg.

She moaned, her fingers tangling in his hair.

On and on, it went. Their movements more fever-ish, the slide of his leg against the juncture of her thighs sending her higher and higher while the brush of her leg against his arousal brought him more fully erect.

Finally, when she thought she could stand no more, he lifted his head and gazed at her. "I want you. Badly."

She shook her head, sanity returning with a *thunk*. "We can't." She started to pull away but he held firm. "We shouldn't even have kissed! I'm writing an article about your company. I need to remain impartial." Not to mention the fact that she had an absolute rule against casual flings; they just didn't agree with the women in her family.

He grimaced. "Believe me, I don't think you've shown any problem remaining *impartial* where I was concerned in the past."

"I don't know what's wrong with me tonight."

He looked into her eyes. "I'll tell you. Bentley Mathison. You were thrown for a loop."

He saw too much, and she still didn't want to talk about it. She gave him a shove, intending to get him to loosen his grip, but instead, she threw off his center of gravity, and he fell backward onto the couch, taking her with him.

They landed in a heap. Her breasts pressed against his chest, his erection nestled against her and their legs tangled together.

She froze. She felt him everywhere, and he felt *so* good. It had been months since she'd had sex, and before that she'd hardly been a swinger. Despite her seemingly glamorous life, a lot of her socializing was work-related.

And now here was Noah Whittaker: Heartthrob. Former racing stud. Playboy millionaire. Scion of one of Boston's leading families. Underneath her. On her couch.

Oh boy. She lifted her head and her eyes connected with his green ones.

The sides of his mouth had teased upward. "If you wanted to be on top, all you had to do was say so." Then he kissed her.

It was easy to kiss him back. After all, gravity was in Noah's favor. All she needed to do was relax—relax into him. It was all too easy.

He didn't grope. He didn't come on too strong or too fast. It was all seamless and smooth. She realized it took a lot of skill to make things seem so natural.

She was barely aware of his fingers slipping up her stockinged thigh, raising her skirt in the process, until his hand slid between her legs and made contact with the spot that was already hot and wet and wanting him.

She felt his touch—light, feathery and quick—and tensed against it. They really shouldn't be doing this.

Still, he was evoking a response from her. She moaned, pressing into his hand. Being with Noah felt delicious, wicked and, yes, forbidden.

"Let go, Kayla," he breathed into her ear. "Let go."

Yes. The whisper of his breath in her ear was the last push that led to her unraveling. She came then, responding to the sure touch of his fingers at her center, the tension of the evening rolling away from her, leaving her sapped and languid.

Slumped against him, she let out a shaky breath, surprised to find tears pricking her eyes, her head relaxing on the curve of his shoulder.

He stroked her back, not saying anything. At some point he caressed her hair, moving the sheet of it back to uncover her face.

She found it all very soothing—tender, really, which was the last emotion that she would have expected to experience with Noah.

"All right, now?" he said, his voice deep, and she felt his question as it rumbled up from his chest.

"Yes," she said quietly. And yet, she'd never been less all right in her life. A lot of things that she'd accepted as fixtures in her life had come unstuck tonight, and there was no putting them back into place.

Over the next few days, Kayla had a lot of time to ponder what had *almost* happened in her apartment on Saturday night and what, in fact, *had.*

Noah had taken down her defenses and had had a glimpse of what lay behind them, and there was no undoing that. He'd just been so *persistent,* but she couldn't seem to find it in her to get mad about it.

She'd also seen a side of him that, she was sure, was rarely on public display. He'd been amazingly kind and concerned when he'd seen her reaction to Bentley Mathison.

The only problem was that along with the newly found peace that had descended on her relationship with Noah came the realization she'd gotten intimately involved with the subject for her news story. A definite no-no in journalism.

And, she couldn't let herself forget, Noah was well skilled at seduction, just like Bentley Mathison had been twenty-eight years ago.

Therefore, there was no doubt in her mind, as she followed Noah around Whittaker Enterprises later that week, that she had to lay down the law: no kissing, no sexual touching and, above all, *no orgasms.* Just thinking about how she'd responded to him on Saturday night caused her to heat.

She jotted notes as Noah kept up a running monologue about nanotechnology, among other things, as they strolled the halls, occasionally stopping to talk to a team leader or other tech employee. The conversations were sprinkled with references to proton-powered molecular biomotors, zero-dimensional objects, quantum computing and entangled particles.

Finally Noah stopped and slanted her a look. "Are you getting all this?"

She looked up from her scribbling. "Yes."

"Great." He looked at his watch. "It's already after six. Want to catch some dinner?"

She took a deep breath. *She had to do this.* "Sorry. I can't."

"How about tomorrow night then?"

She shook her head.

Following him around today had been doing fluttery things to her pulse, not to mention making her all nervous and quivery. Being so close to him now, looking into his deep green eyes, she felt the full force of his compelling charisma, the type of charisma shared by the best sports stars and that sent their fans into paroxysms of screaming worshipfulness.

Plus, now that she'd experienced his warm and caring side the other night, she'd just lost her best defense against him. But resist him, she had to.

"Okay," he said easily, "what about the night after next?"

She took another fortifying breath. "Noah, we—I can't. It would be wrong. I'm here to do a story about Whittaker Enterprises. I can't compromise that. Thank you for being so supportive when I needed a shoulder to lean on after the charity benefit on Saturday night, but what happened afterward…"

"Shouldn't have?"

"Right." This was so hard, especially since she wanted him like crazy, and even though she was *crazy* for wanting him.

He took his time answering, shoving his hands into his pockets. "You should know I don't give up easily. Saturday night something started between us. I don't know about you but I vote for doing some more exploring."

She experienced a little thrill at his words despite herself. *Stop it,* she warned herself. Aloud, she said, "You promised you'd cooperate for this story."

He smiled wolfishly and leaned down toward her. "Yeah, but I didn't promise not to pursue you."

Suddenly she felt as if she'd been caught in a Venus

flytrap. From what she'd already seen, Noah's seduction skills were well honed. And she was weak. *Weak.*

He searched her face, then sighed and straightened. "How much more time did I promise you for this story?"

"Two weeks."

"Okay, you've got them, but after that, sweetheart—" he gave her an intense look "—the gloves come off. You've got two more weeks to finish this story. After that, I'm coming after you."

She should have responded that he could pursue all he wanted—she had no intention of giving in—but the words wouldn't come. Weak. *Weak.* All she managed to say was a lame "But people will think we were involved while I was writing this story, despite all our denials up until now. It'll undermine everything."

He took a step forward and rested his hands on the cubicle wall behind her so that she was trapped between his outstretched arms. Fortunately, it was after regular business hours and most of the staff had already departed.

"Let people think what they want," he said, gazing into her eyes. "I got used to ignoring most of what people say a long time ago."

"But—"

He ducked in for a quick kiss. "But nothing. Are you going to deny you're attracted to me?"

Unfortunately, she couldn't. And, if it was up to her to hold out against jumping into bed together, they were in big trouble.

* * *

Noah made his pursuit of Kayla more dogged as the days passed. He lured her to dinner one night. Two days later, when she was at Whittaker Enterprises again, he coaxed her into having a drink with him after work.

He was fiendishly persistent. But, because he'd promised not to, he didn't put any heavy moves on her—as much as it killed him not to. Now that he'd had a taste of her, he found himself wanting more.

Yeah, she was still a gossip columnist, and he was often gossip fodder. But she was also a leggy blond with a great shape, and he was weak. *Weak.*

Not only that, he liked the way she challenged him, refusing to be cowed. Sometimes, he admitted to himself, he worried about losing brain cells when talking with Huffy, Fluffy, Buffy or any of the rest of them. He remembered Kayla's jibe at the book-launch party about his taste in women, and now he let himself admit that what she'd said may have contained an iota of truth.

Still, he was patient with her. He bided his time. After the night at the Charlesbank Association event, he knew that building trust with Kayla was key. Now that he understood the nature of her relationship to Bentley Mathison, he figured being left by her biological father—even if she was too young to remember when it had happened—had done a lot to influence her relationship with men. Particularly men like him.

So, he pursued her unfalteringly but quietly. On Saturday afternoon, he got her to go out with him to a racetrack near the New Hampshire border where he still occasionally raced cars for fun. She'd tried to demur, but he'd argued it would give her a fuller picture of Noah Whittaker, computer guru.

So, she'd agreed to come along, ostensibly for research purposes, and he'd tamped down the well of satisfaction at having her along. If nothing else, it meant he could keep an eye on her. Because he'd be damned if he held back only to see some other guy take advantage of her availability.

When they arrived at the racetrack, he watched as she looked around. "Do you come here to keep your driving skills honed?" she asked.

"That, and doing a few laps around the track is a good way to blow off steam. It gets my mind focused on something different." He didn't expect her to understand about his love affair with fast cars. Nevertheless, he cocked his head and said, "Want to tag along and find out what it's like?"

"How?" she said. "Don't Indy cars have room only for the driver?"

"There are two-seater stock cars here at the track that they keep for instructors and students." Unlike low-to-the-ground, bullet-shaped Indy cars, stock cars superficially resembled regular cars on the road; they could be modified to include a front passenger seat.

"Didn't you race Indy cars professionally?" she asked quizzically.

He shrugged and gave her a wry smile. "Sometimes I race stock cars down here. I like the variety. Besides, stock-car racing's taken off in the past few years." He slipped his hands into the front pockets of his jeans. "So, are you game?"

She looked at him, then shrugged. "Sure, why not?"

"Yes?" He couldn't keep the surprise out of his voice.

"Mmm-hmm."

"Why?"

"Because you expected me to say no," she said wryly, her lips quirking.

Well, well, he mused. Apparently, his Ms. Rumor-Has-It—he didn't stop to analyze when she'd become *his* Ms. Rumor-Has-It—didn't shy away from a challenge. He found he liked that about her, and he filed the information away for future reference as they went to get the correct protective equipment and wait for their race car to be pulled out.

At the administrative office, they signed the required forms, and then he grinned as she tried on a helmet.

"How's this for a fashion statement?" she asked, amused.

"Would you believe *sexy?*" he replied.

The moment stretched out between them—fraught with need and suppressed desire—until she cleared her throat and said, "We should be getting back outside. The car's ready."

He had it bad. Since when did a woman in a helmet send his temperature shooting up?

When they'd walked back outside and were strapped into the race car, he said, "Last chance to bail. You know, no one will fault you for reporting from the sidelines on this one."

"Forget it."

"If you beg for mercy, I'll stop," he teased.

"Fat chance," she retorted.

He grinned. "Anyway, I plan to go easy for the, uh, virgin riders in the car."

She lowered her visor with a click and, chuckling, he angled the car onto the track.

The ride was like it usually was for him: the next best thing to sex. He accelerated to a cool one-hundred-fifty miles an hour, and they were jostled and bumped as the well-tuned machine roared beneath them and raced over the asphalt. His attention was focused on the racetrack ahead and on every pull and jerk of the car beneath him. Everything else faded into a peripheral blur as he took oncoming turns with smooth calibration, correcting for the car's tendency to head in a straight line.

It was fifteen minutes later when he finally pulled into the pit and stopped. When they got out of the car, he looked over at Kayla. Whatever he'd been expecting to see, it wasn't the grin that greeted him. She looked exhilarated.

"That was great!" she said, still holding her helmet.

His lips quirked up. Not a single one of the women he'd dated had shown any interest in racing, let alone riding in a car with him. The helmet alone would have ruined their hair—but Kayla was apparently a different breed.

"Are you sure you're not a speed addict?" he teased.

She arched a brow. "Oh, didn't I tell you? I *love* roller coasters. I guess *that* was one thing Samantha forgot to mention to you."

Her smile almost undid him. After that, it was a real effort to keep his hands off her. He wanted to make love with her again and again, mate with her, and stamp her as his.

It was crazy to get an acute stab of primal lust just because a woman liked speed, but there it was.

Fortunately, he knew his days of having to take cold showers were numbered. Soon, their remaining week and a half would be up and Kayla would announce she had enough to write her story.

"Really?" Noah said as casually as possible on Kayla's last day visiting Whittaker Enterprises on the following Tuesday.

"Yes," she said. "The article will be appearing in Thursday's paper. I want to thank you for your cooperation."

The way she said that last part had him focusing on her mouth. He wanted to kiss it. Now. He'd been patient, but his self-control had started to ebb.

"No problem," he murmured.

She shifted, seeming suddenly nervous. "Yes, everyone's been very helpful."

"Yeah." He strove to stay focused. "I hope you got enough about nanotechnology and its application to quantum computing."

She nodded. "I've got enough to know you're on the verge of some real breakthroughs here."

He nodded. "Yeah, it'll be great when we finally succeed in making a portable supercomputer."

He realized their conversation was becoming inane, but neither of them seemed able to stop talking. Suddenly struck with an idea, he said, "You know, the development team that just launched that new B-Smart PDA product on the market is going down to the Cay-

man Islands this coming weekend for a few days to celebrate at the firm's expense." At her raised eyebrows,
he grinned. "Yeah, we treat our employees well. We
have to. They're highly skilled, and our competition is
stiff."

"Right," she said, looking like she was wondering
where he was going with this.

"You should come down with us. It'll be a good postscript to the story you're writing and—who knows?—
you may even get another story out of it."

He didn't have to add what they were both thinking:
now that her story was about to be written and filed, her
time was up and the gloves were off. If she came down
to the Caymans, there was a good chance they'd wind
up sleeping together. Pushing his luck where she was
concerned had served him well so far, so he figured the
tactic had a decent chance of working now.

"I don't know—"

"If it makes your journalistic soul feel better," he cajoled, "we've overbooked plane tickets. It'd be no different than journalists riding along on Air Force One
when writing about the President."

She looked like she doubted it, so he changed tactics.
"I've booked a hotel suite. It's got two bedrooms and
two baths." He didn't have to state the obvious: he
wouldn't pressure her to sleep with him, but if the opportunity arose…

"Traveling in style, huh?" she quipped.

He shrugged and said unapologetically, "One of the
perks of the job."

She paused, then said, "Okay."

As he looked into her upturned face, her golden-brown eyes wide and limpid, he knew, as she did, that there was a wealth of meaning behind that "okay," and he planned to explore every nuance of it.

Eight

The Cayman Islands. They'd arrived at the airport on Grand Cayman just after lunchtime, having taken an early morning flight. From the moment Kayla had stepped off the plane, it had been warmth, sunshine and fun wherever she looked. Fun in the sun with Noah Whittaker. She still couldn't believe she'd agreed to come.

Noah had booked the penthouse hotel suite in one of the best island resorts, located right along the well-known Seven Mile Beach. The view from their hotel balcony was of endless ocean, which was bright and inviting in the daylight sun, and, Kayla supposed, dark and mysterious under the moon at night.

Looking down now at the bikini that she was wearing, she wondered whether it had seemed so small when she'd packed it—or whether it had just lost inches while airborne.

She spun in front of the mirror on the bathroom door. As she turned to the side, her gaze came to rest again on the king-size bed that dominated the hotel bedroom.

She'd known from the moment she'd accepted Noah's invitation that they'd wind up *there* together.

Yet, he hadn't pressured her. Instead, he'd taken over the other bedroom in the suite. But she knew, as surely as the sun rose in the morning, they would end up making love.

"Ready?" Noah called from the living room, causing her to jump a little.

She took a deep breath. "Just a minute."

She put on a sarong-like wrap that matched the tropical colors of her bikini, then grabbed her beach bag off the bed.

As soon as she exited the bedroom, any insecurities she had were erased.

"Wow," Noah said, taking her in with one glance.

Her laugh came out sounding nervous to her own ears. He was dressed only in swim trunks, and her pulse picked up.

His hands went to the sides of his head and moved it from side to side.

"What are you doing?"

He gave her a lopsided smile. "Wondering whether I'd come unglued."

She giggled, relaxing a little, and, realizing that was probably what he intended, relaxed even more.

"Let's go," he said, holding out his hand.

She took it—felt her hand encompassed by his bigger, sturdier one—and let herself be tugged out the door.

That afternoon they strolled the beach, taking in the disappearing rays of the sun before eating at one of the finer restaurants on the island.

She loved the local Caribbean cuisine with its emphasis on vibrant seasonings and regional staples such as coconut, plantain and yam. She had mahi-mahi encrusted with herbs and spices and also sampled some of Noah's beef tenderloin stuffed with lobster.

That night, exhausted from a long travel day, she fell onto her bed and was asleep before her head hit the pillow, saving her from making any awkward decision about sleeping with Noah.

The next morning, they woke early and Noah teased her about being out like a light the night before.

"What are we doing today?" she asked, dodging a direct reply to his comment as they ate breakfast at one of the resort's outdoor restaurants.

"Whatever you want. I'm all yours."

And *that* was what she was afraid of, she thought.

Still, she found herself having fun. In the morning, they went snorkeling in nearby reefs. Afterward, they took out a Wave Runner: she clung to his waist as the wind whipped her hair and they raced over the bluest water she'd ever seen.

She supposed she shouldn't have been surprised Noah enjoyed being active: he had the toned and well-muscled body of an athlete. The only surprise was that he combined physical pursuits with the career of a computer geek and the social life of a playboy.

As the day progressed, she found herself dwelling again and again on the contradiction at the heart of Noah Whittaker. Certainly, she'd done him a disservice by focusing on one aspect of his life in her column. She was coming to realize he was a complex, multifaceted man with layers beneath his easygoing facade.

Still, his go-go-go attitude soon had her calling him "Action Man," and teasingly asking whether he ever slept.

His response was to quirk a brow and joke, "According to your column, I spend most of my time in bed."

In response, she'd flushed and resolved not to give him another opening that led into dangerous territory.

Yet, despite having fun, she did find herself thinking back at a point or two during the day to what Ed had said about an illicit offshore company in the Cayman Islands possibly connected to Noah.

Of course, she'd come across no evidence of a connection, and the more she knew Noah, the more she believed a connection to be unlikely. Still, her mind skittered to the fact that she *was* in the Caymans, and if such a connection were to be found, now was the time to try to find it.

At the same time, she knew that finding out anything wouldn't be easy. Given how much secrecy was permitted to companies incorporated in the Caymans, she doubted she could get much information—at least without going down to the government records office herself and attempting to bribe, cajole or lie her way toward gaining access to information. And *that* would also entail lying to Noah so she could sneak away for a while.

No, she didn't have much of a shot. And, then again, there didn't seem much reason to try: Noah had given her a fantastic news story about Whittaker Enterprises. He'd lived up to his end of the bargain. With any luck, that story alone would shoot her career to a whole new level.

She should be relaxing and letting herself bask in the attention of a good-looking guy—just as Samantha had suggested. And, if she were honest with herself, she'd admit Noah was the most fascinating man she'd ever met. She was, in fact, having trouble keeping her hands off him, particularly since, for most of the day, he was dressed in nothing more than his swim trunks.

In the afternoon, they went scuba diving, jumping into the water from the back of a diving boat. They swam together and Noah waved to her, pointing out dazzlingly colored local fish, some swimming in schools. He'd brought along an underwater camera and snapped her picture.

Posing for a photo, she realized with some surprise that, over the past weeks, she'd become immersed in Noah's world and she kind of liked it. It really wasn't as bad as she'd built it up to be.

As their scuba boat approached shore, Noah glanced down at Kayla again. Even in a wet suit, with her hair plastered to her head, she looked great.

He'd done his best to keep his hands off her during

their time in the Caymans so far, not wanting to pressure her. Still, he was experiencing an odd, stir-crazy sensation that was increasing as evening approached.

Yet, while he was going mad with lust, she'd given him no sign that she was feeling similarly…pent up.

When they got back to shore, he asked, "What would you like to do with the rest of the day?"

He prayed she would say something energetic like parasailing, anything to take the edge off his mounting sexual frustration.

"What?" she asked in mock surprise. "No plans for windsurfing or waterskiing? There've got to be plenty of sports that we haven't tried yet."

Yeah, and he could name one that involved a bed, no clothing and plenty of sweaty exertion. Aloud, he said, "Nope. What do you want to do?"

He figured there was practically no chance she'd read his mind and exclaim, *Excellent! Just what I was thinking. Off to bed we go.*

She seemed to consider him, and he wondered for a second whether he'd spoken out loud or she'd picked up something in his expression.

She glanced away. "Hmm."

Was it his fevered imagination or did she seem uncomfortable?

She looked up at him. "Let's go into George Town and take in the shops."

"Great." He figured he did a passable job of looking enthusiastic about window shopping.

When they got into the convertible that he'd rented

at the airport on their arrival, he took the wheel for the short drive to George Town.

Stopped at an intersection, he glanced over at Kayla. She'd been quiet—subdued even—yet tense during the drive so far and, actually, since they'd gotten back from their scuba dive.

Puzzled, and because he was short on patience, he asked bluntly, "What?"

"I want to make love with you," she blurted, then clamped her mouth shut. She looked horrified at the words that had just come tumbling out of her mouth.

Noah felt as if he'd been hit over the head with a sledgehammer. Still, he struggled to appear casual…as if he hadn't been thirsting for this moment…as if, with parched throat, he hadn't just arrived at an oasis in the desert.

Then another thought intruded, and he groaned as he leaned forward and rested his forehead against the steering wheel.

"What?" she asked, sounding startled by his reaction.

"You just realized?" he said, his voice coming muffled to his own ears. "What about five minutes ago? When we were at the hotel and three steps away from a private room?"

She said nothing, and he sat up and hit the gas, turning right.

"What are you doing?"

"Making an illegal U-turn," he said. "Keep an eye out for the police."

A laugh escaped her.

Well, he thought, at least the tension between them had been broken. Now, if only he could get to the hotel room before the last of his self-control dissolved: her admission that she wanted him had already sent it plunging like a runaway elevator.

Out of the corner of his eye, he noticed she was tugging at the neckline of her top and the bikini beneath.

"What's wrong?" he asked, then he tossed her a wicked smile. "You know, I'd love for you to start stripping, but the island has a public-decency ordinance."

She gave an exasperated sigh. "Be serious! I'm just adjusting my bikini. The cups on this one sometimes shift out of place."

"That's right, talk dirty to me."

She laughed. "Hurry."

"What do you think I'm doing?" he asked with mock impatience.

Kayla was amazed at how aware she was of him. If she weren't feeling so desperate, she would have laughed.

Noah had looked thunderstruck at her blurted words. His unguarded reaction had erased any doubts about the response that her declaration would get.

Since their arrival in the Caymans, she'd been waiting for him to make a move, at moments so needy for him that she wanted to scream. Could she be blamed for coming out and saying what she wanted?

She chanced another glance at Noah behind the wheel of the car. He seemed to be driving with a single-minded urgency.

She couldn't believe she'd brought the mighty Noah Whittaker to the edge this way. Then again, not too long ago, she wouldn't have been able to imagine wanting to.

She stifled a nervous giggle.

He took his eyes off the road for a second. "What's so funny?" he demanded.

"You," she said. "Driving as if your life depended on it."

"Laugh while you can." He waggled his eyebrows. "Soon, very soon, baby, you'll be having a different reaction."

"Promises, promises," she retorted, even as she felt her face heat.

He looked at her again as they pulled up in front of the resort. "I can't remember the last time I was this desperate for someone."

Her heart lifted at his words. "Me, too."

They were like two teenagers as they strode across the lobby of the resort and into an elevator.

Once inside their hotel suite, Noah locked the door behind them, gave her a slow smile, backed her up against the wall and proceeded to claim possession of her mouth.

She sighed. He smelled of sand and surf and *male*.

Cupping her face with his hand, he pressed down on her chin with his thumb, opening her mouth wider and sinking more fully into their kiss.

She couldn't get enough of him. Their mouths met, angled, then feasted some more. He sipped at her bottom lip, sucking on its plump softness before his tongue slipped inside her mouth, lazily probing.

The kiss went on and on, gaining urgency as she molded herself to him. She moaned low in her throat, holding him close as the headiness of sensation swirled around them.

When he lifted his head, it was to place light, feathery kisses on her lips, her eyelids and along the curve of her jaw. "Do you know how hard it's been to keep my hands off you until now?" he muttered, his voice husky.

"Mmm," she said, her eyes closed, feeling him everywhere. "Then why did you?"

His laugh held a note of self-mockery. "Trying to prove to you that I wasn't untrustworthy."

She found it hard to think when his hand was kneading her breast through the material of her bikini and sleeveless blouse. "Hmm," she said, opening her eyes. "Seduce me, and I'll let you know whether you've lived up to my evil thoughts."

He laughed softly. "Are you inviting me to do my diabolic best?" he asked, his breath fanning her ear.

"Or worst," she heard herself say even as a voice in her head screamed, *Stop talking and take me!* "It depends on your perspective."

He stifled a laugh. "I don't think I've ever laughed so much while trying to get a woman into bed."

"Neither have I." She tried to clear her head. "I mean, while trying to get a man into bed."

Actually, she couldn't recall ever requesting before that a man make love to her—let alone seducing him into bed—but why quibble with details? Especially when she was concentrating on his hands at the buttons of her blouse, which hit the floor seconds before he disposed of his T-shirt.

She drank in the sight of him shirtless, a familiar sight from the past forty-eight hours, but one she could now openly admire instead of stealing surreptitious looks at. His chest was all hard planes and lean, sculpted muscle, his navel dusted with hair just a couple of shades darker than that on his head.

She let her hands trail over his smooth, tanned skin. "I've been wanting to do this since yesterday," she murmured.

"What?"

"Touch you."

"Yes." He said the word fervently, his hands tightening on her waist. "Touch me."

Below the waistband of his shorts, his arousal pressed against his zipper. She stroked upward.

"Ah, Kayla." The words were torn from him. "I want you so much."

He raked her with a hot gaze as he unsnapped his shorts and let them drop, so that only his swim trunks remained. A second later, he had her skirt pooled at her feet, so that only her bikini was left. "That bikini has been torturing me all day."

She'd never felt sexier than at that moment, knowing he wanted her with a keen need.

Before now, she'd never considered herself the type to make men weak. She knew she had some nice features, and, as a curvy blonde, was some guys' ideal, but she'd always been too straight-laced and serious to consider herself the bombshell type.

Noah, though, made her feel gloriously sexy.

His hands came up to cup her breasts and his thumbs stroked her distended nipples through the nylon of her bikini top.

A moan escaped her and her eyelids felt heavy. Hot, throbbing need coursed through her and settled like a dull ache at the juncture of her thighs.

"Look at me," he said, his voice deep with need. "Watch me make love to you."

She forced herself to focus on his face, which was tight with arousal. He bent his head and sipped from her lips, teasing her, as his hands began to explore her barely-clothed body.

His touch was light and fleeting, yet infinitely arousing. "Your skin is incredibly soft and smooth," he muttered.

"Moisturizer," she said inanely.

He chuckled, then kissed the side of her mouth. "All over?" His hand went to the juncture of her thighs and cupped her there. "Damp," he breathed in her ear.

Her eyes closed. She couldn't help herself. He was doing incredible things to her. His touch sure, deft...wicked.

"And it's got a lovely sun-kissed tone."

"Hmm?"

She heard his husky laugh. "Your skin. It's beautiful, like the rest of you."

Her eyes fluttered open again. "Cuban roots—thanks to my grandmother. I don't need a tan, but getting one will deepen the golden tone. It helps," she said, struggling to stay focused as he continued to rain kisses on unexpected places, "when you need to socialize with the summer-house set…and can't afford a real vacation…and fear sunlamps."

"Ah." His lips trailed across her jaw to her ear. His hand moved, cupped her rear end and brought her snug against him. "Remind me to thank your grandmother."

She moved against him and heard him groan, then gasped as he nibbled at her neck. "Noah…"

He lifted his head, his lips hovering above hers. "You called?" he breathed.

"Yes." Her eyes drifted closed as he bent closer. The kiss, when it came, was searing, deep and demanding.

She didn't know how much more she could stand. She couldn't remember ever wanting someone this much. And he was making sure she was brought to a fever pitch.

When he lifted his head, he looked down at her with hooded eyes, his face a mask of desire. "Now, baby?"

"Yes." She wanted to be joined to him, to know him in the most elemental way possible. "I need you."

"Yes," he muttered. "Oh, yeah." His hands went to her bikini top. He made short work of loosening it, then followed its descent with his mouth, sucking first on one breast, then the other.

She leaned against the wall behind her for support, but her relief was short-lived.

He straightened before her and slipped his hands beneath the band of her bikini panties, sliding her last piece of clothing off her in one fluid motion.

He got rid of his swim trunks then, and she allowed herself a moment to gaze at him. He was big, aroused and ready for her.

She licked dry lips and he half groaned, half laughed. She watched as he reached over to the entry table for the knapsack that he'd dropped there earlier. Reaching in, he pulled out a foil packet.

"Let me," she said, just because she itched to touch him.

He stopped in mid-motion and looked up.

"Let me," she repeated, taking the packet from him.

"Honey—"

She pressed a finger to his lips, not giving him a chance to say more. Then she slowly rolled the protection onto him.

He sucked in a breath.

"There," she said, looking up at him through her lashes, continuing to stroke him. "Done, but not done."

"Oh, we're not done, all right." He took a step toward her, backing her into the wall again. "Now where were we?"

A giggle escaped her and she took a step sideways, then another, inching away from him. "Don't you remember?"

He followed her progress. "It's coming back to me."

She laughed again before turning and making a run for it, dodging his arm as he tried to grab her.

He caught up with her at her bedroom, tumbling her backward onto the bed and coming down on top of her.

They sank onto the mattress together and she was blissfully aware of every inch of him.

"Oh, baby," he muttered, "I've got to have you."

"Yes," she said breathlessly.

And then he was there, probing, stretching her, causing them both to expel a breath when he was inside her. They began to move and set up a rhythm.

It was good, so good. She moaned. "Oh, yes."

"Kayla," he breathed, his face tense with pleasure. "Ah, honey."

She met his thrusts, riding the building pressure until their bodies were damp and sweaty, and still she clung to him.

And then, all at once, she went tumbling over the edge, calling his name as she spiraled into a universe of pure sensation.

He gave a hoarse groan, strained, thrust and seemed to follow her into a realm of exploding stars as he collapsed on top of her.

Nine

Kayla woke up the next morning feeling blissfully used, deliciously achy and thoroughly loved. Only the last gave her pause.

Love?

Sitting up, she looked over at Noah, still asleep, sprawled across most of the bed, the sheet riding low on his chest.

Yes, she *loved* Noah. Not because he'd just given her the best night of her life, though *that* element definitely couldn't be dismissed lightly. Rather, he'd scaled the ramparts even as she'd been manning the fortress of her heart. Underneath the surface of the carefree-playboy image was a guy who continued to surprise and challenge her. He was fantastically smart, teasingly funny and touchingly thoughtful.

That last quality had been on display when she'd run into Bentley Mathison. She'd been feeling vulnerable and weepy, and Noah had been right there to lend comfort and support.

She watched now as he stirred, his lashes flickering as he shifted.

"Hi," she said when he opened his eyes. It seemed like such an insignificant thing to say when her heart felt full to bursting with momentous news: *I love you.*

He smiled slowly and reached for her. "Hi yourself."

Laughing, she attempted to wiggle away even as he pulled her down next to him and proceeded to kiss her thoroughly.

Coming up for air, she glanced over at the alarm clock on the night table. Eleven. "We're sleeping the day away," she protested.

"Really?" he growled against her neck. "I can't think of a better way to spend it."

It wasn't until much later that they got out of bed.

While Noah showered and shaved, she padded into the living room area of the hotel suite in a bathrobe, intent on getting herself some orange juice from the small refrigerator there. She was feeling ravenously hungry.

Passing a console table on the way to the fridge, she glanced down and noticed a couple of legal-sized envelopes. Her eyes skimmed the writing on the top one: it was marked private and addressed to Noah from the registrar of companies in the Cayman Islands.

She paused, her pulse picking up. Despite herself, she inched aside the top-most envelope with her finger and read the writing on the one beneath it: it was addressed to Noah from a law firm on Grand Cayman.

Her mind raced back to what Ed had said to her about rumors of a mysterious offshore company connected to Noah. *A story like that could practically guarantee you the job you want.*

The private letters beckoned and mocked her.

She jumped when the phone rang. She picked it up from the console table next to her. "Hello?"

A tinkling laugh sounded at the other end. "Well, well. I'd heard the rumor but, I confess, I wasn't quite sure I believed it."

Kayla recognized the voice instantly. "What do you want, Sybil?"

She knew her voice sounded brusque, but she didn't care. The puffy little cloud she'd been walking on since waking up was suddenly seeming less buoyant and she couldn't help feeling annoyed at Sybil's intrusion.

"Now, now," Sybil responded, "no need to get touchy."

Kayla guessed that Sybil had called the front desk and asked for Noah Whittaker's room. What rotten luck that she just happened to be the one picking up.

"I called," Sybil continued, "only to confirm what I'd heard through the grapevine—you and our adorable Noah are having a romantic interlude in a tropical paradise. How delightful!" At Kayla's stony silence, Sybil laughed. "I don't want to intrude. I wish you only the best, Kayla dear." Her voice lowered confidingly. "But then I'm sure you're in good hands. Noah has a reputation as a fantastic lover."

Annoyed, Kayla responded, "Is there a purpose to this call, Sybil—other than to bandy about absurd conjectures, I mean?"

When Sybil's voice sounded again, it was cooler and overlaid with false hurt. "Kayla, darling, I'm just surprised, that's all, that you're in the Caymans with Noah. It was the last thing any of us expected, given what he let slip."

"Oh, and what would that be?" The minute the question was out of her mouth, she hated herself for asking.

"Why just that you're his latest fling, dear! You know, I'd said to myself, wouldn't it be delicious if Noah wound up promising a happily-ever-after to his old nemesis in the press? But, no—" Sybil sighed "—Noah corrected me right away. He just laughed and insisted that the day he got serious about you would be the day he'd call himself to feed me details about his private life." Sybil's tinkling laugh sounded again. "Can you believe what a naughty boy he is?"

Kayla felt numb. She wanted to laugh along with Sybil. She wanted to be blasé. *Yes, wasn't it all too funny?* she wanted to say. Instead, a dull ache was growing in the region of her heart. "I'm sorry, Sybil. I have to go," she said, then hung up.

When she'd replaced the receiver, she stood staring at the phone for a minute. She was a fool. A veritable paragon of naiveté.

She began to move around the room—opening the fridge, drinking some orange juice and looking out the window at the bright sunshine—but without taking anything in.

She'd been riding a wave of bliss this morning, spinning fantasies and imagining herself in love, when what she ought to have been doing was asking someone to smack some sense into her.

She and Noah had struck a bargain and, other than for fantastic sex, he hadn't strayed from that deal. Sure, she'd thought something more meaningful was developing between them, but hadn't she also learned that dreamers were losers in the game of love?

She'd heard the story of her mother's youthful indiscretion countless times, yet she'd gone ahead and more or less committed the same mistake herself: fooling herself into believing some wealthy and well-connected guy was interested in her for more than a fling. Her mother had gotten a hard lesson in rejection from Kayla's biological father, and she'd now set herself up for the same thing from Noah.

Hadn't she learned anything from her family history? From her biological father's failure even to acknowledge her?

It appeared not. She was a glutton for rejection.

Coming to a stop again next to the console table, she looked down at the correspondence she'd discovered minutes ago.

She was an even bigger fool for hesitating to read it. Didn't she want to be a hard-nosed journalist? What journalist worth her press pass would turn away from an opportunity like this?

Certainly not one who was going to be dumped after a casual affair. *Certainly not her.*

Drawing forth the sheets from the first envelope, she told herself that once she knew enough, she'd confront Noah.

The contents of the first envelope included copies of a memorandum and articles of association for a company called Medford. Noah Whittaker was listed as the sole shareholder.

She moved to the second envelope and scanned the contents of a cover letter addressed to Noah. The letter advised that an annual return had been filed for Medford and that disbursements to the tune of thousands of dollars had been funneled to the intended beneficiaries.

Perplexed, she scanned the correspondence again, trying to piece together more of the puzzle, when a low sound alerted her to the fact that she was no longer alone.

Raising her head, she found herself staring straight into Noah's frowning face.

Noah couldn't remember the last time he'd felt as good as this morning. Last night with Kayla had been great. No, more than great. They'd made love, fallen asleep and made love again...and again. It had been fantastic.

Which was why, as he emerged from the bedroom, he had a hard time processing the image that confronted him: namely, Kayla looking guilty as hell, holding a sheet of paper and standing next to the console table where, he now recalled, he'd absentmindedly left sensitive correspondence yesterday.

Damn. He felt his smile vanish.

"What are you doing?" he asked, having already formed an opinion but hoping to have it contradicted.

Kayla's chin came up. "Shouldn't I be asking *you* that question?" She held the paper out to him. "What is this?"

He felt his lips tighten as he moved toward her. "You went through my mail? You were snooping?"

How many times had he had to deal with invasions of his privacy? Photographers who'd put their high-powered lenses right up to the windshield of his car? Reporters who'd go into restaurants he'd just left and bribe other diners into divulging what he'd eaten and what he'd said?

"I'm a gossip columnist, remember?" she responded coolly. "Prying is my job."

What the heck was wrong with her? She was a far cry from the warm and willing woman that he'd held in his arms last night. In fact, she was acting like those colleagues of hers in the press who were the bane of his existence. *She'd* been the bane of his existence until recently.

"What the heck is that supposed to mean?" he asked, pulling the paper out of her hand. Glancing down and realizing it was the letter from his lawyer, he forced himself to tamp down on his temper. No one was supposed to know about Medford and his involvement with it. He'd gone to great lengths to ensure that.

"What do you think it means, Noah?" she demanded. "Did you expect me to set aside my journalist's instincts just because you arranged to have a little fun in the sun with me?"

He went stony. He'd had women slap him with less sting. "Right. Excuse me for thinking your career ambition might come second to loyalty to friends—or *lovers*."

She laughed cynically. "Loyalty? And what would you know about that?"

He reached across her and grabbed the rest of the correspondence off the table. "Enough to think you'd be satisfied with our bargain and the news story that I'd fed you," he bit back. "Obviously, I was wrong."

She folded her arms. "And I suppose your concept of loyalty is flexible enough to encompass a love'em-and-leave'em philosophy?"

"What are you talking about?"

"Sybil LaBreck just called," she said, as if that explained everything.

"Yeah?" He thought for a second. "How the heck does she know we're down here?"

"We gossip columnists have our ways."

"You don't say."

She nodded. "Sybil seemed quite happy to have the rumors of our romantic idyll confirmed by my picking up the phone in the hotel suite that's booked under your name. She was just—how did she put it?—*surprised*." She added, her voice dripping acid, "After all, you'd told her that the day you got serious about me would be the day that you called her yourself with a story for her column."

He had some vague recollection of running into Sybil at the Charlesbank Association charity event. She'd been irritating and had asked probing questions. She'd hinted that she suspected he and Kayla were really having an affair and not just attempting to bury the hatchet for appearance's sake. He recalled saying something dismissive in order to get rid of her. And now, it seemed, that *something* was coming back to haunt him.

Still, he wasn't going to try to explain to Kayla that the comment had been made half-jokingly in an attempt to make Sybil go away. Because what counted was that Kayla hadn't trusted him.

She hadn't trusted him enough to give him a chance to explain what he'd said to Sybil. If she'd trusted him, she wouldn't have sneaked into his private correspondence.

It was clear that she valued getting a story more than any feelings for him. And, given his experience with the press, he was ten kinds of sucker for ever thinking otherwise. Even if they'd made the earth move last night.

He held up the correspondence that he clutched in his hand and demanded, "You want to know what these papers are about?" When she made no reply, he continued, "I'll tell you—the worst ten seconds of my life."

She looked taken aback.

"That's right," he said. "The racing accident I'd give anything to undo."

She shook her head. "But those papers refer to a company called Medford."

"Right. The company that I formed for the sole purpose of supporting Jack's family since the accident."

"But that's a good thing…"

It gave him perverse satisfaction to see she seemed perplexed. "What? Are you disappointed you haven't discovered another scandal connected to me? Did you think I didn't know there'd been rumors—despite doing my best to keep Medford under wraps—that I was involved with a mysterious company in the Caymans?"

"But why create an offshore company? Why try to hide the fact that you're doing something good because…?"

He arched a brow. "Because, instead, people might believe I'm doing something bad? Is that what you were going to say?" He shrugged. "I didn't want Jack's family to know who was helping them."

"But why?"

She was pressing him for answers that he wasn't prepared to give. She had a journalist's doggedness all right and at the moment he was finding it damn irritating. "I just preferred it that way," he said, adding sarcastically, "is that okay with you?"

She unfolded her arms and looked shocked. "You still carry an enormous amount of guilt about the accident, don't you? Do you blame yourself?"

"What is this? Pop psychology 101?" he snapped.

He could swear a flash of hurt crossed her face. Well, that made two of them with open wounds.

"I was just asking."

"No, you were asking *and* snooping." The betrayal cut like a knife. She was prepared to sell him out for a moment's glory in the newspaper and a shot at a better job. Hell.

He turned his back on her abruptly.

"Where are you going?" she asked.

"To pack," he said curtly, not looking at her. Today was supposed to be their last day in the Caymans anyway. Might as well pack it in early. "It was fun while it lasted, honey, but now it's over."

Noah shoved his hands in his pockets and paced to the windows of his office, where he stared out unseeingly.

Surly. That described him to a T lately.

After the debacle with Kayla in the Caymans, he'd been mad as hell. He should have stayed mad as hell. Instead, he'd started to invent reasons to see her point of view. Had started to think maybe he was partly to blame.

Which was crazy. Just as crazy as the fact that he'd trusted a reporter to begin with. He needed his head examined.

To top it off, Sybil LaBreck was hot on their trail again. Her most recent headline, just after his return from the Caymans, had shouted: Is Noah Whittaker Finally Getting Paired Off? Sybil went on to detail his and Kayla's getaway in the Caymans despite his recent denials that anything romantic was going on.

He thought back to his face-off with Kayla in the Caymans. If he hadn't been so pissed off, he might have tried explaining to her about his comment to Sybil. At the time he'd tossed off the remark, all he'd wanted was to throw Sybil off the scent—because he'd already started lusting after Kayla intensely.

And the sex, when it had happened, *had* been incredible. Hotter and steamier than he'd fantasized. It had been good. *They'd* been good.

His mind went to the question that had been chewing at him more and more: was it fair of him to have expected Kayla to check her reporter's instincts at the door of their hotel suite?

That was precisely what he'd expected, he realized. Because of the sex, because he'd started wanting and needing her and because she'd gotten under his skin.

But, even if he had a right to be angry because she hadn't trusted him more, *he'd* been the one to leave the Medford correspondence lying around. And—he could now concede, putting himself in her shoes—Sybil's call had led her to believe he was an untrustworthy jerk.

"Troubles?"

He turned from the window and saw Matt standing in the open doorway to his office. "No more than usual."

Matt came in, shutting the door behind him. "Yeah, well you haven't been your usual self lately, and people have started to notice."

He shrugged as Matt sat on a corner of his desk. "We all have a bad week occasionally."

"Yeah, and yours happened to coincide with your return from the Caymans with Kayla Jones. Don't think people didn't notice."

"So, let people notice."

Matt shook his head resignedly. "Stashing a sexy reporter in your hotel room during a firm trip to the Caribbean?" Amusement darkened his brother's eyes. "Probably a first even for you."

"I'm usually not that stupid." Or gullible.

"Oh, I don't know about that," Matt drawled. "You've got a well-known weakness for hourglass blondes."

"Did you just come in here for a comedy break? Because, if that's the case, I don't have the time. I've got deadlines." Deadlines he didn't give a damn about at the moment and couldn't seem to get focused on trying to meet anyway. He walked over to his desk and started shuffling paper.

Matt hopped off and turned to face him. "Want to tell me about it?"

"In a word? No." Then he added, because he couldn't let it go at that, "She's all wrong for me."

Matt shook his head. "Doesn't matter."

Noah's head jerked up and he asked incredulously, *"Doesn't matter?"*

"Yup, you've got it bad, little brother. Resistance is futile."

"Yeah, right."

Matt sauntered toward the door, turning back when his hand was on the knob. "Call me when you're ready to acknowledge the power of the force—the *female* force, that is. In the meantime, stop trying to wipe the floor with everyone who crosses your path around here."

"Right, thanks," Noah grumbled.

Matt nodded his head. "Great. I'll consider the advice delivered then."

When his brother had gone, Noah dropped the papers he was holding. Matt knew nothing about it. Still, he'd give it another week. With any luck, he'd be able to get a grip for that long. Then he'd consider his options.

The weekend after their return from the Caymans, Kayla was moping. Ultimately, she and Noah had wound up taking different flights back to Boston because she was able to get on standby on an earlier flight. And, frankly, the urge to flee had won out over the impulse to stay and appear unmoved.

Because when Noah had said it was over, she knew he didn't just mean their mini-vacation in the Caymans. Their ill-advised affair was over, too.

On Saturday, Samantha called and asked if she could crash on Kayla's sofa bed that night because she'd be in Boston to catch a concert. The next morning, Kayla found her already awake in the living room, Samantha having let herself in late the night before with a spare key.

Samantha took one look at Kayla's face and guessed something was wrong. Though she got peppered with questions, Kayla dodged most of them. The confrontation with Noah was still too fresh and ugly.

Instead, she faced her computer screen and forced herself to edit a story for work. However, by lunchtime she'd given up. She'd edit a sentence and find her mind wandering, replaying and analyzing the argument with Noah and questioning her judgment.

She wondered now if she'd been too suspicious and had jumped to conclusions. Maybe she should have questioned him before opening the letter, instead of deciding to confront him afterward. And, given Noah's history with the press, she supposed she shouldn't have been surprised that he'd been annoyed when he'd caught her prying.

At that last thought, she stopped short. What was she doing? Maybe it had been wrong to look at his mail, but she was still a reporter—one who'd been doing a story on *him* and Whittaker Enterprises. Sure she'd been incensed by Sybil's phone call, but he hadn't denied treating her as no more than his latest blonde and letting everyone know it.

And, to add insult to injury, he'd had the nerve to make her fall in love with him.

She was an idiot.

She dropped her head against the computer monitor, then hit her forehead repeatedly.

"Kayla, what are you doing?" Samantha asked with a mixture of exasperation and amused alarm.

Before Kayla could answer, the apartment buzzer rang.

"I'll get it!" Samantha said. At the intercom, Kayla heard her say, "Who is it?"

"Allison Whittaker," came the reply.

Kayla raised her head and Samantha said, "It's—"

"I heard," Kayla responded, then sighed. "Tell her to come up."

Ten

When Allison entered the apartment, she said, "Sorry to drop in on you like this without warning."

"It's okay. It's a Whittaker trait that I'm already familiar with," Kayla said dryly.

Allison gave Kayla a knowing look as she shrugged out of her leather jacket. "My husband thinks I'm crazy for coming." Samantha reached for her jacket and Allison stuck out her hand. "Hi. I'm Allison, Noah Whittaker's younger sister."

"I'm Samantha, Kayla's little sister," Samantha replied, taking the outstretched hand. "Glad you're here. She's been in a funk all morning."

Allison broke into a toothy smile. "It's always the baby sister to the rescue. What would they do without us?"

"Dunno. I ask myself that all the time."

"Samantha!" Good grief, Kayla thought, did her sister have to tell the Whittakers everything? "And I was *not* in a funk."

"Yes, you were. I heard you. Under your breath, you were saying that word that's a one-letter difference from *funk*."

Kayla rolled her eyes. Wasn't she entitled to feel a little blue every once in a while?

Noah's sister stifled a grin. "I wish I'd had a sister when I was growing up. Instead, I got the Marx Brothers—Chico, Harpo and Groucho."

"Which one's Noah?" Samantha asked as they went into the living room.

Allison cast them a sidelong look. "At the moment, he's definitely Groucho."

Kayla felt a strange thrill go through her. Covering the sudden feeling of discombobulation, she asked, "You stopped by because…?"

"I'm paying it forward."

At Kayla's confused look, Allison waved a hand. "It's a long story. Let's just say, we Whittakers like to assist each other, whether the help is wanted or not."

As Allison sank into the armchair, Samantha joined Kayla on the couch and said, "So, Groucho. Noah. Interesting."

Kayla shot her sister a wide-eyed quelling stare.

"Yup, Noah's been hard to live with," Allison said. "Or, I should say, hard to work with."

"Does he know you're here?" Kayla asked, then immediately wished she hadn't done so.

Allison shook her head. "No, and he hasn't confided in me either. Except, when I stopped by his office the other day, he got stony and monosyllabic when I mentioned Sybil's headline about the two of you in the Caymans together. He claimed nothing was going on, at least not anymore."

Kayla dropped her gaze.

"But," Allison continued, "I know *something* must be going on. Apparently, the word around the office is that Noah's been miserable to work with recently. Even Quentin and Matt have noticed it." She shrugged. "I put two and two together and came up with your address, but let me know if I'm wrong."

"Is that why you're here?" Kayla found herself asking, unwilling to give a direct reply.

Allison tilted her head and looked at her for a second. "Isn't it obvious why I'm here? I love my brother and he's miserable."

"And you think I'm the cause of it?"

"No, I think your leaving is the cause of it."

She wished Allison was right, but Allison didn't know how badly things had ended between her and Noah. She'd felt raw and weepy all week. And Allison and Samantha's understanding looks only made things worse. Suddenly emotional, she blinked rapidly.

"Want to tell us about it?" Allison asked sympathetically.

Kayla took a deep, uneven breath and waited for her

emotions to subside. Then an explanation of everything—
well, almost everything—came tumbling out of her.

She detailed how she'd gone down to the Caymans,
had answered Sybil's phone call and had wound up
looking at Noah's private correspondence, following
which she and Noah had argued.

She didn't go into the fact that she'd woken up all
starry-eyed after a torrid night twisting the sheets with
Noah. She'd replayed *those* scenes enough times in
her mind.

When Kayla was done talking, Allison looked like
she wanted to ask more questions about what Kayla
had read in Noah's mail, but resisted the urge. Instead,
she sighed. "My brothers. What they don't know about
women I could write an encyclopedia about."

"What?" Kayla said, even though she'd heard perfectly well.

"I knew one of Noah's flippant comments would get
him in trouble one day." Allison shook her head. "I
mean, anyone can see he's hooked on you. Anything
he's said to the contrary is just evidence that he's a fish
realizing he's been caught on a hook."

Kayla tried to picture Noah as a fish caught on a line
and failed.

"Well, I've always thought Kayla had an issue with
trusting men," Samantha said, "and that it all went back
to Bentley Mathison."

Now it was Allison's turn to say "What?"

Kayla shook her head. "Samantha's a psychology
major. She's been reading one too many self-help books."

"Have not. Nobody in our family wants to listen to logic, that's all."

"What's any of this got to do with Bentley Mathison?" Allison put in.

Kayla shrugged in resignation. "He's my biological father."

"Wow," Allison said.

"I don't broadcast the fact," she said dryly, "and he doesn't know about our connection." She gave Allison a brief rundown on her mother's encounter with Bentley Mathison twenty-eight years ago.

Allison raised her eyebrows. "No wonder you looked shook up at the Charlesbank Association event."

"Was it that obvious?" Kayla said, startled.

"Well, you did look a little frazzled. That's the moment when I thought there was something going on between you and Noah. He acted all protective and concerned."

Kayla shook her head. "Maybe, but I wouldn't attach too much weight to it."

Allison gave her a shrewd look. "You know, Noah has plenty of faults. He can be too damn self-assured for his own good—"

"Yes, I know."

"But he's true to his word. He'd never have organized Whittaker Enterprises into a major force in the computer field if he hadn't been driven and good with the follow-through."

Kayla nodded. She knew that, of course.

She paused. Or did she?

Despite the fact that Noah had made sure to drive home to her that he wasn't like her biological father, when put to the test during their stay in the Caymans, had she fallen into the trap of thinking Noah was like Bentley Mathison?

Sure, there was a superficial resemblance to her biological father: both men were wealthy, possessed charm in spades, were successful with women, and had drive and ambition.

But Noah hadn't failed her. He'd kept to every single promise he'd made to her, including giving her unfettered access to Whittaker Enterprises.

In the past several weeks, she'd also come to realize he wasn't the pampered playboy she'd liked to portray him as in her column. He was way more complex than that.

And the truth was, if she'd been in his shoes and had had his history with the press, catching someone *she'd* just slept with snooping into *her* private correspondence would have made her crazy mad, too.

She looked at Samantha. "On second thought, maybe I ought to concede that you have a point."

"Of course I do!" her sister exclaimed.

She bit her lip. "What should I do?" she asked of no one in particular, the words just slipping out.

"That's up to you," Allison said.

"You know," Kayla said, uncertainty still gnawing at her, "he didn't even try to explain about his comment to Sybil."

"Typical," Allison responded. "He was probably so pissed off you'd jumped to the worst conclusion that he figured he shouldn't have to explain." She looked from Kayla's face to Samantha. "It's just the two of you? No other siblings?"

Kayla nodded.

"Right," Allison said briskly, leaning forward. "Listen, I grew up with three brothers, and I learned a few things. The male mind has two guiding principles—don't explain and don't ask for directions."

"You're kidding me," Samantha said laughingly.

Allison winked. "There's a self-help book waiting to be written there. Keep it in mind."

"Well, what do you think I should do?" Kayla asked. She wanted to believe Allison was right.

Allison stood up. "I'll leave that up to you. You'll think of something. Noah deserves a second chance, even though he's done nothing to explain himself. Trust me—I've seen the way he looks at you." She added, "It would be nice if life were smooth. The truth is, though, sometimes we come to a gap in the road and we just have to jump and hope for the best."

Trust, Kayla thought. Did she dare put it into play where Noah was concerned? But then, what choice did she have? She was in love with him. Who'd have thought?

When he got to work, Noah reached into the in-box on his desk and turned over a plain legal-sized envelope. There was no return address, yet suspicion curled within him. Later, he'd say it was an indefinable aura: the presence of *her.*

He slid his finger under the flap and, once he'd gotten the envelope open, two sheets came tumbling out.

It was the final draft of an article with Kayla's byline. The headline caught his eye immediately: Noah Whittaker's Secret Life Revealed. At the bottom of the first sheet, scrawled in ink, was a note that the article would be appearing in that day's edition of the *Sentinel*.

He froze.

She wouldn't. She hadn't.

Yet, his gut already told him otherwise.

Anger coursed through him. Hadn't she done enough to him? She'd wrung him out like a used washcloth and hung him out to dry.

Evidently, however, he was worth one more story, he fumed, and she was going to squeeze every bit of news that she could out of him.

He forced himself to read the article.

There was a description of his racing crash and its immediate repercussions. The article went on to discuss how Noah had gone back to the computer-technology field after leaving racing and had joined the family business, which he'd built into a major competitor in the computer field.

He read on, looking for and expecting an exposé of his secret involvement with Medford.

Instead, the article discussed how, contrary to his public image as a high-living playboy, Noah was a well-respected and hard-working entrepreneur who also had his eye on helping others—even if they didn't know that they were being helped.

That was it. No mention of Medford. No mention of the Cayman Islands. Nothing. The article concluded by saying that the author had discovered that Noah was much more complex and likable than his public image might have let on.

Noah put down the article and grasped his head in his hands. He knew without question who had sent the article to him. And now he knew why.

He'd believed Kayla to be treacherous. Now he found himself revisiting and revising that judgment.

He hadn't been able to forget her. In the past couple of weeks, he'd been in a foul mood, grousing to his brothers and cracking the whip with his subordinates. In general, he'd been a pain in the ass.

All because he'd been missing her. Wanting her.

Loving her.

He stopped.

Love. Was that what it was, this feeling of having his guts wrenched out of him, stomped on and shoved back into him upside down? This dull ache that he carried with him like an attaché case cuffed to his wrist?

Sure, he'd had the hots for a number of women in the past. He'd had crushes and, later on, serious cases of lust. He'd even had a couple of whirlwind affairs.

But none of those women had sucker-punched him, whipping the wind out of him the way that Kayla had. Certainly no one had gotten under his skin in the same way. No one had peeled away the layers and no one had kept on digging to get beneath the playboy facade.

He was glad it had been Kayla who'd finally done it and discovered the essence of him.

He raised his head, a wry smile tugging at his lips. With a sudden thought, he pulled open his desk drawer and found the photograph he'd tossed in there two weeks ago.

Kayla. She was smiling and happy and carefree in the Caymans—the best romantic idyll of his life. Her bikini molded the body that he'd come to know so well and that still made him ache at night.

Suddenly, he knew what he had to do. It was time for a call to Sybil LaBreck.

Out of habit, Kayla turned on her computer at work and clicked on the link on the *Boston World*'s Web site that brought her to Sybil LaBreck's column. Reading the headline, she nearly spewed her coffee. She set down her cup and dabbed at the hot liquid that had spilled when she'd jerked her arm away from her mouth.

Her eyes caught again on the headline: Ms. Rumor-Has-It Rumored to Have Gotten Noah Whittaker: Sweethearts to Walk Down the Aisle.

In all the times she'd read Sybil's column, she'd often been amused, sometimes annoyed, at being scooped, and occasionally disbelieving. This was the first time, however, that she'd been totally shocked.

It couldn't be! She'd never known Sybil to make things up out of whole cloth, but she supposed there was a first time for everything.

She forced herself to scroll down and read on: "Noah bought a four-carat sparkler for his honey."

She skimmed the article until her eyes came to rest on a quote purportedly from Noah himself: "'It's not an ark, but there's a twenty-foot yacht that I want to sail into all of our tomorrows with Kayla by my side.'"

Damn, damn, damn. She'd demand a retraction!

Sybil was in for one heck of a tough time. She'd be publicly embarrassed once it came out that what she'd printed wasn't true. And, of course, Noah could and probably would threaten to sue Sybil's socks off.

At the thought of Noah, she stopped.

She hadn't heard from him since she'd sent him a copy of her article. What was he thinking? He definitely wouldn't be happy about *this*—being linked in Sybil's column to her, a woman that he'd come to despise.

Unless, of course, he believed she was the source for Sybil's story? She dismissed the thought right away, then retrieved it. He wouldn't think so, would he?

She picked up the phone. There was only one way to answer that question. She dialed Whittaker Enterprises.

When she got through, Noah's secretary advised her that Noah was in a meeting. When Kayla asked when she could reach him, she was told he'd be out of his meeting within the hour, but then he'd be heading to the airport for an afternoon flight.

Not stopping to think, she grabbed her purse. She had to nip this story in the bud *today,* and that meant speaking with Noah *now.* They had to decide what to say when reporters inevitably started calling, not to mention how to curtail any more ridiculous stories from Sybil.

In addition, she promised herself, she was going to say her piece to Noah. Explain and apologize. Afterward, if he had her escorted off the premises by security guards, so be it.

Just as she slipped into her tailored jacket, however, she caught sight of Ed coming toward her, and groaned.

Ed slapped the copy of the *Boston World* that he was holding against his palm, his expression one of bemusement. "So," he boomed, his voice audible across the newsroom, "you've been holding out on us, Jones."

Kayla looked around. Because it wasn't even nine in the morning, the newsroom was mostly empty. Kayla sent up a prayer of thanks that her newsroom dramas seemed to occur before the office really got hopping.

To Ed, she said, not even pretending not to understand, "I know this will be hard to believe, Ed, but trust me. I'm not involved with Noah now, nor was I when I wrote that first story about Whittaker Enterprises."

She stopped to take a breath and Ed said, "Kid, one of these days I'm going to tell you how I met my wife while covering the biggest story of my career. Let's just say, a study in journalistic ethics it ain't."

She must have looked flummoxed, because Ed shrugged. "Hey, we're all human. Just keep your old newspaper friends in mind, will you, when you're schmoozing with the bigwigs?"

"Ed—" She stopped and shook her head. There were no bigwigs in her future, but she'd settle for keeping her job. All her explaining could come later, however, so instead she said, "Thanks, Ed," then took off down the hall.

She had a plane to beat.

Eleven

When Kayla got off the elevator at Whittaker Enterprises, she found Noah speaking with his secretary.

Just in time, she thought, then wondered whether what she felt was panic or relief. She barely had time to wipe clammy palms on her pants, however, before he looked up and caught sight of her.

"Hi," she said as she walked toward him. He looked delectable and she fought the urge to launch herself into his arms.

He turned to face her, shoving his hands in his pockets. "Hi."

"Can we talk?"

He nodded. To his secretary, he said, "Hold my calls."

"Right," the secretary replied, looking from Noah to Kayla speculatively.

When he'd ushered her into his office and closed the door, she took a deep breath and then plunged right in. "Have you seen Sybil's column today?"

He gave her an odd look. "Should I have?"

"Her headline claims the two of us are about to walk down the aisle!" Right away, she felt her face heat with embarrassment.

He arched an eyebrow.

"I just wanted to let you know that I had nothing to do with it."

"I didn't think you had," he said smoothly.

Relief seeped through her. "You didn't?"

"No." A wry smile curved his lips.

"I don't know who her source was, but—"

"I do."

"What?" *What?*

"I know who her source was."

He did? Well, no wonder he seemed so calm.

"Her source was very reliable," he went on. "He was totally trustworthy."

"Oh, right," she said crossly. "How reliable could he have been if he was totally mistaken?"

He cocked his head and gave her an inscrutable look. "How do you know he was wrong?"

"Because—" she spluttered. He was going to make her spell it out for him? "Because you...I..."

"Yes?"

"We're not getting married!" she exclaimed.

"Ah."

"Anyway," she said, changing the subject from a dangerous topic, "would you mind telling me who the source is?"

"A guy I know," he said enigmatically.

"A 'friend' of yours?" she asked disdainfully.

"He's a good guy," he countered. "Somewhat misunderstood and occasionally misguided, but well-intentioned."

"Uh-huh." He'd had the nerve to condemn her for being a gossip columnist, and yet he was all too ready to forgive a friend who'd run to the press with untruths. "Good guy, right!"

"Hey, you might hurt his feelings," he said, though he didn't look worried.

Far from it, actually. She paused as a touch of suspicion intruded. "How long have you known this friend?"

"Years. That's why I can vouch for his character."

Her suspicion grew and, with it, confusion. Was he playing with her? Did he believe he hadn't exacted enough retribution for her apparent betrayal in the Caymans? Was he angry about her news article and was this his way of punishing her? Or…?

She searched his face. He didn't look angry. If anything, he looked…expectant.

Her heart began to thud. "I'm surprised you're such good buddies with someone who'd run to the papers with details of your private life."

He held her gaze as he said, "Let's just say my friend's learned that society columns can serve a useful purpose."

"Really?" Well. "I didn't ask. Have I met this friend of yours?"

He took a step toward her. "You know him."

Her heart beat faster. "Is he good-looking?"

"Very." He took another step toward her.

"Oh." He was within touching distance of her now, and she was aware of every inch of him. "Smart?"

"I guess so."

"Funny?" Could that breathless voice be hers?

"Some say so."

"Oh."

"Why do you ask?" he asked, his voice low and husky.

She swept him a glance from beneath her lashes. "I may be in the market for a steady date."

A smile tugged at the corners of his lips. "Oh? That's too bad."

Her eyes opened wide. "Why?"

He shrugged. "Because I guess that means you won't be interested in this," he said, pulling something from his pocket.

He held it up, and the radiance of the diamond caught and reflected the light.

She gasped and lifted her gaze from the ring to his face.

"I was the source, Kayla. Because I love you, and I've been an ass."

He went down on one knee.

"Oh!" She felt tears threatening, then felt like an idiot for being able to manage only a half-coherent exclamation.

He took her hand, slipping the ring onto her third finger, as he gazed up at her. "Will you marry me?"

She looked at him through a sheen of tears. "I love you, too," she warbled.

His smile stayed in place. "I think the appropriate answer to that question is 'yes' or 'no.'"

He was joking, but his words were endearingly tinged with uncertainty.

"Yes!"

He rose then and folded her into his arms. The kiss that he gave her was soul-searchingly thorough, and she gave herself up to it.

She couldn't believe her luck, couldn't fathom how her dreams had come true. But, at this moment, she was content to revel in the fantasy turned reality.

Between kisses, she asked, "You planned this?"

"Mmm," he muttered before diving for her mouth again.

A moment later, she tried again, "I can't believe you planned this!"

He raised his head and smiled. A slow, intimate, caressing smile. "You know what they say, desperate times call for desperate measures. Sybil was only too happy to help."

Her eyes widened. "You mean you went to Sybil for help—"

He nodded, his smile widening. "She was quick to point out that I'd be eating crow." He added, his voice tinged with sheepishness, "You'll recall that I once said something to the effect that the day I got serious about you would be the day I'd call her myself with details about my personal life. Well, I can't imagine getting more serious about you than I am now."

"That's—" she began, then stopped as a thought intruded. "Your flight!" She looked around. "What time is it? You're going to miss it!"

He threw back his head and laughed.

Puzzled, she asked, "What's so funny?"

He managed to look sheepish and pleased with himself at the same time. "Er…"

Her eyes widened. "There is no flight, is there?"

She tried to slug him playfully but he caught her up in a bear hug. He kept laughing while she squirmed.

"All right," he admitted finally, "I convinced my secretary to say that I had a flight to catch. I was betting— no, hoping—you'd see the headline in Sybil's column and want to get to the bottom of the gossip right away. Just in case, though—" his guilty look deepened "—I decided to give you an extra reason to think you needed to come racing over here."

She looked at him. He'd gone to a fair amount of trouble. For her. She melted. "I suppose that explains why you were carrying an engagement ring in your pocket?"

"Yup."

"You move fast," she said laughingly. "Not that I'm complaining."

His mouth quirked up on one side. "I like speed, remember?"

She just gazed at him, this wonderful, funny, sweet

guy who'd taught her about trust, laughter and love. "I owe you an apology."

He loosened his hold and cocked his head. "For what?"

"For not trusting you more." She paused. "I thought you were just like Bentley Mathison because you have money and social status. I singled you out to be a favorite target of my column."

He rested his forehead against hers. "If it weren't for that column of yours, we would never have met." He gave her a quick kiss. "I'll always be grateful to Ms. Rumor-Has-It."

"You've done a major about-face," she teased.

"Well, I've learned a few lessons, too."

Now it was her turn to look interested and surprised.

He cleared his throat. "You were right that I've been a little rudderless since the accident." He shrugged. "I was torn up over Jack's death. The way I chose to cope was by turning to models and actresses and partying."

"And now you've turned to gossip columnists," she said impishly.

He cupped the side of her face, running his thumb over her lips. "I've discovered that gossip columnists have their charm, and that they have a difficult job, just like most other people."

"They're charming even when they dredge up the past?" she asked, unable to resist.

"Yeah," he said, holding her gaze. "Even then. Especially then."

Her heart lifted.

"I was wearing Jack's death like an old and familiar

shirt. I thought I had come to terms with it to some extent because I'd been rendered blameless by the official investigation and I was doing what I could to help his family." He paused for a few seconds. "I didn't realize how much I was still waiting for an absolution—until your article."

She nodded. "I was hoping you wouldn't be angry."

"I was when I first saw it, but then I actually took a look at what you'd written. Reading the article, I think I finally gave myself permission to forgive myself."

"I wanted to make amends," she said, "even though I thought I'd destroyed any chance of a relationship between us. And by the way, thanks to my story about Whittaker Enterprises, you're now looking at the newest business reporter at the *Sentinel*."

Noah laughed, then lifted her up and hugged her before setting her down again. "Fantastic!"

She knew she had a ridiculous grin on her face.

"So, who's taking over as Ms. Rumor-Has-It?"

"With any luck, Jody Donaldson and *not* my sister. Samantha has this ridiculous idea that the column is the way to meet guys."

"I like your sister. She's spunky."

"Well, don't worry, she's ready to welcome you into the family with open arms."

"Mine already thinks you're great for taking me down a peg or two," he teased, then got serious. "Speaking of family, what do you intend to do about Bentley Mathison?"

"Nothing." She thought a minute to figure out how

to express how she felt. "He obviously decided long ago not to have anything to do with my life, and, now that I've met him, I don't think I want to have anything to do with him either. And I've decided to stop beating up on myself for being genetically related to him. Genes are not destiny."

"Good," he said, appearing satisfied. "There's no use getting upset about things that you can't change, but realize there's a lot that you *can*."

"I love you," she said. He knew her so well. This was what she'd yearned for...dreamed of. Noah understood her, so well, in fact, that she saw herself better.

A glint entered his eyes. "Want to demonstrate?"

Her eyes widened. *"Here?"*

He looked around the room. "Hmm," he said, "maybe you're right. We've only got the couch and the desk. It'd be better if we go to the firm's bedroom."

"The firm's bedroom?" she echoed, sure that whatever he was suggesting was scandalous.

His eyes crinkled. "Unofficially and euphemistically known around here as the *private* conference room." He winked. "It's a room for use by employees who are pulling a late night and don't have time to go home and catch some shuteye. But—" he leaned forward confidingly "—and I guess it's all right to share this with you since you're no longer Ms. Rumor-Has-It—it's been rumored to have been used for clandestine rendezvous."

Her gasp ended in a laugh. "No, we couldn't! People will see us!"

He waggled his brows. "Not if we're careful."

She started to protest again, but he grasped her hand, tugging her along.

Outside the office, she couldn't bring herself to look Noah's secretary in the eye as they passed her desk and Noah said, "I'll be out for a while, Maureen. Take messages, and ring me on my cell if the office is burning down."

They rode the elevator down a floor, anticipation and sexual energy crackling between them. When they exited and strode along the corridor below, Noah nodded to and acknowledged a couple of people as they passed. However, no one seemed to pay any particular attention to them.

When they turned a corner, Noah cast a quick look up and down the hallway before opening the nearest door and ushering her into a dimly lit room. He closed and locked the door behind him.

She looked around. The room was furnished with a double bed, a night table, a desk and a TV, and came equipped with its own bathroom.

She couldn't believe they were doing this! She nearly jumped when Noah slipped his arms around her from behind and nuzzled her neck. "Someone will hear," she said weakly.

"Don't worry," he said in a low voice. "This room has some soundproofing—an extra drywall to keep noise out—" he placed a kiss on her neck "—and in."

"Oh."

His hands stroked just below her breasts. "Though," he murmured, "we should probably try to keep down the decibel level."

"Think about your reputation in the office," she cajoled halfheartedly as his hands slid beneath her top and under her bra to cup her breasts. "If someone hears us…"

She trailed off as his hands caressed her.

Behind her, he was hard and hot. He blew into her ear. "Thanks to you, my *reputation* makes me the great seducer. I might as well try to live up to the title, don't you think? Where's the fun otherwise?"

Right. Of course.

The longer he kissed and caressed her, the more sense his logic made. In fact, he was starting to sound like a veritable genius…. She turned in his arms and pulled his head down to her for a hot kiss.

Soon his suit jacket hit the ground, followed by her top, and his shirt and tie.

He traced her cleavage along the contours of her lacy black bra. "Pretty," he murmured before divesting her of that item as well.

He slid his undershirt over his head and she trailed her fingertips over his flat, muscled chest and along the biceps of his arms.

Love had liberated her to admire him openly and desire him unabashedly. He was gorgeous and he was all hers.

The look in his eyes when her gaze connected with his again was filled with desire. "You're invited to touch me anywhere…and everywhere."

His words shivered over her skin, making her nipples tighten and the heaviness between her legs increase. She itched to be surrounded by him, consumed by him.

He bent and placed a kiss at the corner of her mouth. "Of course," he said, "I expect reciprocal privileges."

She heated at the thoughts that conjured.

He pulled her close then, and she gave herself up to a kiss that seared them both. The evidence of his need fueled her own.

When they broke apart, he said, "I've got to be with you," and she could only think he'd given voice to her own need.

Quickly, they pulled off the rest of their clothes.

When he was gloriously naked, she reached out and stroked his erection, and he sucked in a breath. She watched as his eyes closed, his face a mask of need and desire and pleasure.

"You know we're going to have a fantastic life together, don't you?" he said hoarsely.

"Mmm-hmm," she responded as she continued to stroke him, then added teasingly, "is this the fantastic part?"

Without waiting for a response, she dropped down and took him in her mouth, stroking and caressing him, hearing his hissed intake of breath.

"Oh, yeah," he groaned. *"Kayla."*

She took her time and, when she was done, she stood up and met his passion-clouded eyes.

"Wow," he said hoarsely. Then he picked her up and tossed her on the bed. She let out a squeal but he cut it off with a swift kiss.

He trailed kisses down her body, blazing a trail of tingling sensation that caused her to shift restlessly. When he reached the juncture of her thighs, she whimpered.

"Shh," he whispered, his breath hot against her.

"Easy for you to say," she whispered back as his hands caressed her thighs.

"Trust me," he said soothingly.

And she did. In the deepest, truest sense, she realized, as he kissed her intimately, sending sparks shooting through her.

Her hands tangled in his hair. "Oh, Noah…"

When she thought she could stand no more, he lifted his head and reached for the pants that he'd discarded at the foot of the bed, then pulled out a small foil packet. He quickly donned protection, then stretched out next to her, gathering her into his arms.

She felt seductive, making love clandestinely with the man that she loved while wearing only the beautiful, sparkling engagement ring that he had given her.

He moved over her, seeking entry, and she shifted to accommodate him. She sighed as he slid inside her, and he expelled a breath that was half groan, half moan.

Then they moved together, loving each other and building to a crescendo that had her quivering and clinging to him.

"I love you," she gasped.

"Likewise," he replied on a groan.

She could feel the tension building within her, the world dimming. She knew she was close.

"So, is it enough?" he whispered in her ear, his breath coming heavily.

"More than I ever dreamed," she responded, and that was her last thought as she went tumbling over the edge along with him…and into their future.

Epilogue

"**W**ho would have guessed Matt would be the last Whittaker standing," Noah said in disbelief. "The rest of us were running around trying to take each other out of the game while he just sat back and watched."

Allison nodded in agreement. "The fiend."

"Yeah," Noah joked. "To think he had the nerve to thwart your grand scheme to marry off all your annoying older brothers so you could rule the world."

He and Kayla, along with Elizabeth and Quentin and their baby, had shown up at Allison and Connor's townhouse in the Beacon Hill section of Boston to watch the New England Patriots take on the Pittsburgh Steelers in one of football's more heated rivalries. After his recent marriage to Allison, Connor had put his luxury condo on the market and moved into Allison's townhouse, though they had kept Connor's house in the Berkshires as their getaway home.

It was a blustery Sunday afternoon in November, and they were all sitting around Allison's family room, baby Nicholas asleep upstairs, waiting for the football game to start. Matt would have been there, too, but he'd begged off, citing an early dinner with some business associates.

"Matt plays his cards close to his chest," Quentin said. "We'll never know whether being the last unmarried Whittaker was his goal all along or whether things just happened that way. As we all know, Matt's always been sort of enigmatic."

"Well, I think it's time we got Matt to his happily-ever-after," Allison said. "After all, I tried to get you and Noah married off, and, Noah, you and Quentin helped me get married off. We practically owe it to Matt. I, for one, consider it almost my duty."

Noah and Quentin groaned in unison.

"What?" Allison demanded.

Noah and Quentin exchanged looks before Noah said, "Let's just say sometimes we wish you'd stop taking the sisterly loyalty thing to its illogical extreme."

"Ha, ha," Allison retorted. "The fact of the matter is, we have to do something—"

"And you're not above enlisting my help and Quent's," Noah finished.

Allison lifted her chin. "I'm not above making strategic alliances."

He snorted. "You're also not willing to concede defeat."

"The fact of the matter is," Allison said, ignoring him, "Matt doesn't stand a chance. I'm not above some scheming, and you and Quentin obviously know something about snagging a lifelong partner to head down the aisle with."

Noah cast her a skeptical look. "Just *how* are we supposed to get Matt shackled? He's notoriously private. I'm his brother, and I don't even know if he's seeing anyone."

Allison glanced over at Kayla. "Kayla would know. She gets the dirt on a lot of people."

Noah turned to gaze at Kayla, too. As usual, just looking at her made him feel good. Her hair was pulled back in a ponytail, and her ice-blue turtleneck contrasted nicely with the creaminess of her skin. He thought again about how much he loved her. "You know," he said, "you never did tell me who tipped you off about me for your column."

"Um." Kayla's eyes strayed to Allison.

Noah followed her gaze. "Don't tell me," he muttered.

Allison stopped with a glass raised halfway to her lips. "Don't flatter yourself."

Noah arched an eyebrow.

"Oh, all right." Allison made a dismissive gesture with her hand. "I may have said at a cocktail party or two, *There he goes! Go get 'im!* But only because I didn't want Kayla sniffing around *me* for a story."

"So you'd throw your own brother to the bloodhounds?" Noah asked in mock offense.

"No," Allison said archly, "but I'd feed him to the single women in the room." She looked from him to Kayla. "And I don't see you complaining."

He looked again at Kayla. He'd found love in the most unexpected place, but it worked for him. With her help, he'd put the past behind him instead of trying to forget it with an endless stream of women and parties. Though he and Kayla came from different backgrounds, it was like finding the other half of himself: *the better half.*

He dropped his arm onto Kayla's shoulders, pulling her to him. "Have I been complaining, Kayla?"

Kayla looked at the man who'd opened her eyes to a whole other level of closeness. Thanks to him, she'd learned that rejection and hurt and distrust weren't the inevitable consequence of loving someone who'd grown up in better circumstances than she had, just as she'd learned that those same circumstances of birth were the least important aspect of her relationship with Noah.

She looked now into Noah's green eyes, so happy that she was nearly giddy, and so secure in his love that she could tease right back. "Mmm, no complaints, but I'm spreading the word to Jody Donaldson and Sybil LaBreck that your title of Boston's most eligible bachelor should be passed on to Matt. As far as I know, he isn't seeing anyone."

Allison laughed.

Noah raised his eyebrows. "Honey," he pretended to plead, "don't tell me you're taking a cue from Allison and using the society pages for matchmaking."

Kayla smiled at him, while Quentin and Connor

joked about Noah joining the "married men's club," and Liz said, "Hear, hear!" in approval.

"You know what they say," Kayla said sweetly, just before Noah's lips claimed hers, "you can take the girl out of the gossip column, but you can't take the gossip columnist out of the girl."

* * * * *

Silhouette®

Desire®

**From *USA TODAY*
bestselling author**

Annette
Broadrick

THE MAN
MEANS BUSINESS

(SD #701)

When a business trip suddenly
turns into a passionate affair,
what's a millionaire and
his secretary to do once
they return to the office?

Available this January from Silhouette Desire

HARLEQUIN *Super Romance*

HOME TO LOVELESS COUNTY
Because Texas is where the heart is.

MORE TO TEXAS THAN COWBOYS

by Roz Denny Fox

Greer Bell is returning to Texas for the first time since she left as a pregnant teenager. She and her daughter are determined to make a success of their new dude ranch—and the last thing Greer needs is romance, even with the handsome Reverend Noah Kelley.

On sale January 2006

Also look for the final book in this miniseries
The Prodigal Texan (#1326) by Lynnette Kent
in February 2006.

Available wherever Harlequin books are sold.

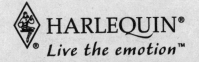

HARLEQUIN®
Live the emotion™

COMING NEXT MONTH

#1699 BILLIONAIRE'S PROPOSITION—Leanne Banks
Battle for the Boardroom
He wants to control a dynasty. She just wants his baby. Who will outmaneuver whom?

#1700 ENGAGEMENT BETWEEN ENEMIES—
Kathie DeNosky
The Illegitimate Heirs
Sometimes the only way to gain the power you desire is to marry your enemy.

#1701 THE MAN MEANS BUSINESS—Annette Broadrick
Business was his only agenda, until his loyal assistant decided to make marriage hers!

#1702 THE SINS OF HIS PAST—Roxanne St. Claire
Did paying for his sins mean leaving the only woman he wanted…for a second time?

#1703 HOUSE CALLS—Michelle Celmer
Doctors do not make the best patients… Here's to seeing if they make the best bedmates….

#1704 THUNDERBOLT OVER TEXAS—Barbara Dunlop
She really wants a priceless piece of jewelry, but will she actually become a cowboy's bride to get it?

SDCNM1205